Marcus followed Kinsley, then stopped short when he heard fabric rustling. He glanced around, looking for signs that they weren't alone.

"What's wrong?" she asked, heading back in his direction.

He heard the soft click of a gun safety being removed and knew what was about to happen.

He shouted for Kinsley to get down and threw himself in her direction as the first shot exploded. He landed on top of her, covering her body with his as a bullet slammed into the ground nearby.

He pulled his firearm, aiming toward the shrubs. "Police! Put your weapon down!"

There was a flurry of movement and then silence.

Kinsley had been attacked twice in one night. Her house had been set on fire while she was in it.

Was Randy Warren trying to silence her?

Marcus needed to find him.

He needed to stop him.

And he needed to make certain he wouldn't have a chance to come after Kinsley again.

Aside from her faith and her family, there's not much **Shirlee McCoy** enjoys more than a good book! When she's not hanging out with the people she loves most, she can be found plotting her next Love Inspired Suspense story or trekking through the wilderness, training with a local search-and-rescue team. Shirlee loves to hear from readers. If you have time, drop her a line at shirlee@shirleemccoy.com.

Books by Shirlee McCoy

Love Inspired Suspense

Hidden Witness
Evidence of Innocence

FBI: Special Crimes Unit

Night Stalker
Gone
Dangerous Sanctuary
Lone Witness
Falsely Accused

Mission: Rescue

Protective Instincts
Her Christmas Guardian
Exit Strategy
Deadly Christmas Secrets
Mystery Child
The Christmas Target
Mistaken Identity
Christmas on the Run

Visit the Author Profile page at Harlequin.com for more titles.

EVIDENCE OF INNOCENCE

SHIRLEE MCCOY

LOVE INSPIRED SUSPENSE
INSPIRATIONAL ROMANCE

LOVE INSPIRED® SUSPENSE
INSPIRATIONAL ROMANCE

ISBN-13: 978-1-335-72240-9

Recycling programs
for this product may
not exist in your area.

Evidence of Innocence

This edition published by arrangement with Harlequin Books S.A.

For questions and comments about the quality of this book, please contact us at CustomerService@Harlequin.com.

Love Inspired
22 Adelaide St. West, 40th Floor
Toronto, Ontario M5H 4E3, Canada
www.Harlequin.com

Printed in U.S.A.

I know that thou canst do every thing,
and that no thought can be withholden from thee.
–Job 42:2

To my parents, who always let me dance to my own rhythm and sing to my own tune. I would not be the person I am without you. *Thank you* just never seems enough.

ONE

Wedding cake number 3. Delivered.

Kinsley Garrett put a bright blue line through the last item on her daily to-do list, dropped the check she'd been handed in an envelope with the rest of the day's payments, and shoved the key into the ignition of the van.

Now she just had to make the nightly deposit.

That meant driving back to Frenchtown in an aging Chevy Astro with four balding tires. She could call her boss, Doris Green, and tell her that she would make the deposit in the morning when the weather cleared and the roads weren't coated in ice and snow, but the cash from the bakery's register was in the envelope, along with three hundred dollars from the cookie delivery she had made to a retirement village in Missoula.

"Better to *not* have it in the house all night. You don't want to be responsible if something happens to it," she murmured.

Flakes of snow and specks of ice splattered the windshield as she pulled away from the reception hall. The lot was nearly full, the wedding reception just getting started. The bride and groom had been pleased with the cake. Doris would be happy with their glowing praise and promise of an excellent online review.

Kinsley didn't worry about those things.

She worried about making sure the money she collected matched what was deposited in the bank. She worried about keeping her reputation in Frenchtown, Montana, as pristine as the snow that tipped the mountains to the west. She worried about bringing the bakery back from the brink of financial ruin, helping Doris get into the position to sell it for a nice profit so that she could finally retire.

She worried about finding the person who had murdered her father.

Eighteen years was a long time for justice to be deferred.

And fifteen years had been a long time to spend in prison for a crime she hadn't committed.

Images flashed through her mind. Blood splattered on white walls. A gun. Her father as he had been the last time she had seen him: lying in a pool of his own blood.

She shuddered, pushing the memories away.

She eased the van onto the main road that ran from Missoula to Frenchtown. On a good day, the drive took twenty minutes. This was not a good day. Unlike Florida where she'd grown up, Montana had long brutal winters and bitter weather. In the two and half years she'd lived there, Kinsley had learned to drive on icy snow-coated roads.

That didn't mean she liked it.

She turned up the heat, knowing the effort was futile.

The delivery van was twenty-three years old, limping along on its last legs because Doris didn't want to invest in a new one. That was fine. Kinsley was there to help, not take over. She owed a huge debt to Doris, and she would do whatever it took to repay it.

Neither of her grandparents had lived long enough to see their efforts to free Kinsley pay off. Doris, her late grandmother Adele's best friend, had stepped in when they were gone. When Adele had passed away three years before Kinsley's exoneration and release from prison, Doris had continued to the fight for justice until Kinsley was finally freed. If paying back that debt meant driving an old van and working at Flour and Fancies Baked Goods until Doris was able to sell it, she'd do it.

The rest, she'd figure out when the time came.

What she would do with her freedom now that she finally had it, where and how she would live the rest of her life could be figured out later. After Doris had settled into retirement.

She slowed as she rounded a steep curve in the road, windshield wipers flicking ice and snow from the window as the van crept forward. Headlights appeared in her rearview mirror. Another lone traveler heading from Missoula to Frenchtown. There was nothing else in this direction. Just more small towns dotting the northern edge of the state.

Not a place she had ever imagined living.

But here she was.

For now.

She eased around another curve, the headlights still in her mirror. Up ahead, she could see a few scattered lights. Frenchtown sprawling past its boundaries, farms speckling the landscape. A few houses here and there, set off from the road, long driveways winding through fields or forests. Another few minutes and she would reach town, drive to the small bank, make the deposit, go home.

Same thing she had done every Saturday for two and a half years. She didn't mind the routine. Every day of her life in prison had been regimented and scheduled. There was some security in that. No matter how much she hated to admit it. She had learned lessons during her incarceration. Some of them served her well. Others, she preferred to forget.

A man darted into the road, a black smudge against the glistening asphalt. She slammed on her brakes, clutching the steering wheel as the van spun out, bounced off the road and hit a thick fence post. The abrupt stop stole the breath from her lungs and, for a moment, she sat still, staring out the window and into the remnants of last year's cornfield.

Someone banged on the window.

She jumped, her heart slamming against her ribs.

A man stood outside, his face nearly touching the glass, his eyes wild. Coat hanging limp from a scrawny frame. Gaunt cheeks. Wild eyes. Blood on the hand he'd pressed to the window.

"Are you okay?" she asked, swinging the door open and hopping out of the van. "Did I hit you?"

"Yes," he said, his gaze darting to the road.

The vehicle that had been behind her had pulled over and was idling quietly in the breakdown lane. An SUV. Dark-colored. A man got out. Instead of approaching, he stood back, watching as the scene unfolded.

The hair on Kinsley's arms stood on end and

her mind screamed that something was very wrong.

"There's a house just about a half mile from here. I'll go get help," she murmured, trying to ignore the fear creeping up her spine and lodging in her skull. She suffered from PTSD. She had major anxiety. She panicked about things that didn't need to be panicked over. People ran into the road without looking. Cars pulled over when traffic accidents happened. For all she knew, the guy had already called 9-1-1 and was just waiting for help to arrive.

"Get back in the van." The man she'd hit grabbed her wrist, his fingers digging painfully into her skin as he climbed into the vehicle and scrambled over to the passenger seat.

She was yanked sideways, her head glancing off the edge of the doorframe, her body off balance. The van's engine was still running, exhaust puffing into the air. Snow and ice still fell, coating her hair. The world was carrying on as it always did, but something very wrong was happening.

"The van isn't going to make it back onto the road. I'm going to walk to the nearest house for help," she said, trying to pull away.

He yanked her forward, pulled a gun from beneath his jacket and pointed it at her heart. "I said, get back in the van."

Her stomach dropped, her heart racing as she complied. She left the door open, knowing that running was her only real option. If she drove away with him in the van, she wouldn't survive. She had taken self-defense classes—at her therapist's suggestion, to help ease her anxiety—after she'd arrived in town. She hadn't expected to ever need what she'd learned.

Whatever you do, don't get in a vehicle with your attacker, had been drilled into the participants' heads.

"Close the door and drive!" he shouted.

Kinsley froze with fear and indecision. Running from a gunman had seemed like the easy choice when she'd been in the self-defense class. Now, it was the most difficult thing in the world.

Jump out and risk being shot? Or stay and risk the same?

"Close it!" He shoved her toward the driver's door with his gun hand, the butt of the semiautomatic smacking her cheek as he tried to force her into action.

Blood dripped onto the frilly white apron Doris insisted she wear at the shop and during deliveries. Splotches of red on white and she was back in time, sneaking into the quiet house, certain her father was sleeping soundly in his bed. She hadn't realized what she'd tripped over. Not at first. She shuddered, pushing the memory away. If she didn't act, she would end up like her father had. That couldn't happen. Not before she saw justice done.

She jumped out of the van, terror fueling her.

He shouted, and she expected to hear a gun report, feel a bullet slam into her back.

The fence post she'd hit was in front of her, taut barbed wire stretched to either side of it. Five feet high and spiked with ice-slick hooks. She clambered over, ignoring the tear and rip of flesh and fabric as she tumbled to the other side and jumped to her feet. Her coat caught and she shrugged out of it, running hard for the house she knew was at the northern end of the field.

She reached the edge of the cornfield at a dead run. The house was straight ahead, security lights turning on as she ran up a hill and into the yard.

She was close. So close!

Something slammed into her side and knocked her off her feet. She fell, the breath knocked from her lungs. She fought, twisting onto her back, kicking, screaming, doing everything she had been taught to do in class.

But he was bigger, stronger, his body stretching over hers, forcing her deeper into grass and ice, one hand grabbing both her wrists, pinning them above her head, his legs trapping hers, his body preventing any movement. She bucked, desperate to free herself. Desperate to get away.

"Stop," he said quietly. Gently. Nothing like the harsh shout at the van. "I don't want to hurt you more than you already are."

Not the same voice.

Not the same man?

She stilled, her heart beating so fast, she felt sick and dizzy with it. Breath heaving. Body going into full-out panic.

She couldn't breathe. No air reaching her lungs. Just painful dry gasps.

"It's okay," the man said, easing away. "You're okay." He shrugged out of his coat and covered her with it.

"What's going on out there?" a woman called. "You okay, Marcus? Should I call the precinct?"

"Call an ambulance," the man answered.

He was crouched in front of Kinsley. Not touching her. Just watching. Curly black hair. Dark skin. Hazel eyes. Five-o'clock shadow. She knew him. Had spent five Tuesday evenings in the self-defense class with him.

Marcus Bayne. Frenchtown's chief of police.

She'd have said his name, but she still couldn't catch her breath. She scrambled to her feet, dizzy and disoriented. Nervous. For reasons that had nothing to do with being chased through the cornfield.

She didn't do well around police.

She had spent the past few years doing everything she could to avoid contact with them.

She took a step back.

"Don't run," he commanded.

She froze. The past—never far away—edging in again. She couldn't be arrested. Wouldn't be. She knew how that could end. She had lived it.

She pivoted and tried to run.

He was too fast, grabbing her arm and yanking her around.

"I said don't run," he repeated calmly.

"Let go of my arm."

"Not until we agree that you're not going anywhere. Do we?"

She nodded stiffly, everything in her demanding that she do exactly what he was telling her not to.

She had been locked away for too many years. She'd missed sunlight and balmy air and the scent of summer foliage. Just thinking about it made her go cold with dread.

"Let go of me," she muttered. "Please."

Marcus didn't want to scare the woman more than she obviously had been, but he wanted answers, and he wanted them fast.

The ferocious barking of his dog, Fitz, had brought him out onto the front porch. He'd seen a person running toward the house, and his instincts from four years in the Army's special ops unit had kicked in. He'd tackled the trespasser first, realized she was a woman later.

A woman with a long red braid and bangs that fell into her eyes. He knew her. He'd taught a women's self-defense class that she'd attended. The back edge of his three hundred acres bordered her property. They didn't run in the same circles, and he didn't see her very often, but Kinsley Garrett was definitely *not* a stranger.

"Kinsley, right?" he asked, keeping his voice calm and light.

She nodded, her body stiff, her stance defensive. "Yes."

"Garrett?"

"You taught the self-defense class I took. I'm sure you know who I am, Chief Bayne," she replied, looking him straight in the eye.

"Marcus," he corrected. He only went by Chief Bayne when he was on duty. "Want to tell me why you're on my property?"

"I was being chased. I wouldn't have trespassed otherwise."

"Chased by who?" he asked, ignoring her comment about trespassing.

"I don't know. I was driving into town and a man ran in front of the van. I hit the brakes and ended up off the road."

"It's not a good night for braking hard," he commented, scanning the area behind her, looking for signs that someone else was nearby.

He saw nothing.

Sensed nothing.

Fitz had quieted.

"It also wouldn't have been a good night to run over a pedestrian," she responded, her voice shaking.

"True. You said you were being chased?" he prodded, anxious to get the full story and to act on it.

"When I opened the door to ask if the pedestrian was okay, he tried to kidnap me." Her hands were shaking as she tucked a strand of hair behind her ear, but her voice was calm. There was a gash on her cheek and a bruise on her head. Her clothes were torn, hands bloody. The results of an attempted kidnapping? Or something else?

He had no reason to doubt her, but he had been lied to before. He had been a police officer for too many years to take everything he heard at face value.

"We struggled," she continued. "I got hit in the face with the butt of his gun, and—"

"He had a gun?"

"Yes."

"Did you get a look at is face?"

"Yes." She offered a quick description. Male. Caucasian. Dark hair. Very thin. It could have been any one of dozens of people in town, thousands of people in Missoula.

"Can you tell me where this took place? How far from here? I'm going to call in for some help. I want to get his guy off the street."

She offered the information quickly.

He pulled out his cell phone and called it in.

His family was in the house.

He had an entire town that depended on the police department to keep criminals off the street and to keep its citizens safe. He had a description of the perp, but a name would be even more helpful.

"Was he someone that you know, Kinsley?" he asked.

"No."

"You're sure? No ex-boyfriend? Husband? A regular at the bakery, maybe?"

"Chief... Marcus, if I'd seen him before, I'd remember. He was a stranger." She emphasized *stranger* as if she were afraid he didn't believe her.

"I'm not challenging you. I'm just asking questions so that we can rule things in and rule them out."

"You can rule out any connection to me. I've never seen him before."

"All right."

She nodded stiffly, her lips pressed together, her jaw tight.

He had been in law enforcement since he'd left the military. First, as a patrol officer in Missoula. Then as chief of the Frenchtown police department. After nearly fifteen years on the job, he knew when a witness or victim was nervous around law enforcement.

Kinsley Garrett was.

He had no idea why. She hadn't caused any problems since moving to town. As far as he knew, she'd never even gotten a speeding ticket. "Once the ambulance and patrol cars arrive, I'll head down to the road. See if the van is still there or if it's been taken. It's possible this was a carjacking. The guy got what he wanted and left the scene."

"A carjacking? You've seen the Flour and Fancies delivery van, right?" she asked, pacing to the edge of the porch and staring out into the front yard. "Who would want it?"

"Someone desperate for money or—"

"The money! The daily deposit is in the van!" She darted off the porch and probably would have run to the road if he hadn't snagged the back of her coat.

"Hold on a minute. You can't go running off

to look for money after you were nearly kidnapped," he said.

She whirled around. "How am I going to tell Doris that I lost the daily deposit?"

"You aren't. You're going to tell her that it was taken. If it was."

"I hope you're not implying that I made all this up," she said.

"I was stating that if the money was taken, that's what you'll tell Doris. We haven't seen the van. We have no idea if it's still there."

"Why else would someone jump in front of the van, except to steal the money?" she asked.

"To kidnap you?" he suggested.

He didn't want to scare her more than she had been, but he also didn't want her running off without a thought to what might happen. He knew how quickly normal life could become a nightmare. He'd lost the love of his life to violent crime. She had been murdered while he'd served his last tour in the military. Their wedding had been planned, her dress had been fitted. He had spoken to her hours before her murder. They had both been excited for the next phase of their lives.

It had never happened.

Her murderer had never been caught.

When he'd decided to become a police officer, his aunt Winnie had asked if Darcy's murder had had something to do with the choice. It'd had everything to do with it. He had no regrets about his decision.

"Why would anyone want to do that?" Kinsley asked as he helped her back up the porch stairs.

"You are an attractive young woman. Sometimes that is all the reason a predator needs." He held her arm as she settled on the porch swing.

"I'm worried about the deposit," she admitted. "Doris can't afford to lose money from the business."

"Like I said, as soon as the ambulance and a police officer arrive, I'll look for the van."

"I appreciate at that, but I'd prefer you go now."

"I'd rather not leave you here alone," he said.

"I won't be alone. Your daughter is keeping me company."

"Daughter?" He swung around and caught a quick glimpse of Rosemarlyn peering out one of the narrow windows beside the door. She ducked away, and he could imagine her scurrying back up the stairs and into her room. At seven years old, Rosemarlyn was a handful. Inquisitive, busy and often bored, she kept him on his toes. "That was my niece."

"She's staying with you?"

"Permanently. My sister passed away a year and a half ago. I became her guardian."

"I'm sorry. About your sister. Not about you having your niece. I'm sure she's lovely."

"Depends on the day and who you ask," he murmured, opening the door and shouting up the stairs, "You had better be in bed, young lady!"

"Is she up?" Aunt Winnie hurried from the back of the house, her dark curls springing wildly. Just ten years older than Marcus, she had stepped in when his parents had died in a car accident. He had been eleven. His sister, Jordyn, had been twelve. Winnie had been a college student, working toward a teaching degree. She had given that up, moved in with Marcus and Jordyn, and finished the job of raising them.

"She was at the window," he responded, raising his voice to be heard about the wail of an ambulance that was racing toward them.

"I'll take care of her. You do what you need to," Winnie said.

He closed the door and turned to watch as the ambulance parked and EMTs jumped out. A police cruiser pulled in behind the ambulance and a female officer hopped out. Charlotte Daniels was one of the newest members of the Frenchtown police. Driven and eager, she had a reputation among her fellow officers for being unapproachable and cold.

Marcus didn't care about her interpersonal relationships at the office. He cared about how she did her job. She was excellent at it, her compassion and empathy for victims of crimes and her desire to see justice done had given her a reputation in the community as being one of the best officers on the squad.

That's what he wanted.

It was what he cared about.

He knew what it was like to be on the other side of crime. He knew the helplessness, anger and fear. Because he had lived it.

"Chief," Charlotte called as she jogged toward him, "what's going on?"

He explained quickly.

"You want me to go to the scene and cordon it off?" she asked, her gaze shifting to Kinsley. She was surrounded by EMTs and barely visible. "Or get a victim statement first?"

"You handle the victim statement and call in a couple of the other squad cars. Have them meet me on the road. I want to see if there's any evidence to collect."

"I'm sure you're aware that you're not on duty," she responded.

"I'm always on duty."

And that was part of the problem Rosemarlyn was having with her adjustment to life in Frenchtown.

Or so her second-grade teacher, the school counselor, the principal and vice principal had said the last time he'd been called in for a meeting.

Since then, he had been spending more time at home. He had been doing everything he could to make certain his niece understood that she was loved and wanted. But, she was precocious, busy, and a little too smart for her own good. No matter what he tried, she still managed to get into trouble at school.

He jogged around the side of the house. His SUV was parked next to Aunt Winnie's Jeep. After Jordyn's death and Rosie's—Rosemarlyn's—arrival, she'd come to stay for a month. Three months later, she'd moved into the apartment above the garage. She had been there ever since.

Having her around was a tremendous help, but Marcus felt guilty for relying on her so heavily. She had attained a teaching degree in her thirties, and was now teaching fifth-graders at the elementary school Rosie attended.

Winnie called it a God-thing, that she could be there for her great-niece the way she had been for her niece. But Marcus thought she deserved to live her life, to do her thing, to find all the happiness she could without the burden of someone else's child. At forty-five, Winnie had never been married or had children of her own. Unfortunately, her fiancé had dumped her when she'd stepped in to help him with Rosie.

The amount of guilt he carried over that was incredible.

Work was an escape from Rosie's rambunctiousness and from his guilt. Even if he hadn't been off duty, he'd be heading to the current crime scene. As chief of police in a small town, he was expected to be on scene when serious lawbreaking occurred. A near kidnapping fit that category. Frenchtown wasn't known for its violent crimes and violent offenders. It had its fair share of petty criminals, but a stranger kidnapping was unheard of.

He didn't know much about Kinsley. She had moved to town three years ago, bought the property that abutted the back edge of his three-hundred-acre spread and moved in without fanfare or introduction. She worked at Flour and Fancies. She didn't cause trouble. She kept to herself.

She was nervous around law enforcement.

He didn't think she was hiding any information regarding the incident she'd reported, but he couldn't be sure. It was possible this wasn't a stranger kidnapping. Maybe she was protecting the perp. Or maybe she was afraid of the consequences of revealing an identity.

Marcus's job was to uncover the truth, to find the guilty party, and to make sure dues were paid for the crime. Criminals needed to be off the street, and he was devoted to making sure that happened as quickly as possible.

Once he got a look at the scene, he planned to have another talk with Kinsley and to get the entire story out of her. No matter how reluctant she might be to tell it.

TWO

Kinsley didn't feel comfortable around the police.

She didn't enjoy talking to them.

Frankly, she didn't trust them.

Despite all the good she knew they did, anxiety filled her every time she saw a police uniform. Being in an interview room, waiting to be questioned, only compounded the feeling.

She should have agreed to be transported to the hospital, but she hadn't wanted to go there, either. She had wanted to return to her house, to call Doris and explain the situation, and then get on with her night. Her therapist, Emma Danby, had told her avoidance wouldn't solve her problems or rid her of the PTSD that had plagued her since the night she'd found her father's body.

But avoiding seemed safer than facing her fear.

Fear?

Terror was a better word.

Her heart beat frantically as she paced the small room she'd been brought to. She had been asked questions and then shown photos of criminals fitting the description she had given. To her surprise, the man who had attacked her had been among them. She recognized his face immediately. His thin build and narrow features. She had slid the photo across the table, assured the officer that he was the man they were looking for and had hoped to be released to go home.

Instead, she had been asked to wait.

Kinsley had agreed because she hadn't dared do anything else. She'd been afraid she would somehow implicate herself in another crime she hadn't committed. If the deposit money was gone, if the van had been stolen, she didn't want to be accused of being part of that.

A plot to get her hands on money to support her drug habit and her expensive lifestyle.

The prosecuting attorney in her father's case had said that so many times during the trial, the words seemed etched on Kinsley's soul.

She had been a wild child. She had dabbled in things she shouldn't have. She had snuck out to go to parties with older friends.

But she would never have murdered her father.

And yet she had been accused and convicted of the crime.

Her exoneration—fifteen years after the fact—couldn't ease the sting of betrayal she had felt. By the system, by family members, by her friends.

The door opened and Marcus Bayne stepped in. He closed the door behind him, offered a quick smile before gesturing to a chair. "Have a seat, Kinsley."

She did as she was told. Fifteen years of incarceration had taught her to obey orders immediately and without question. Even three years after being released, she struggled to make decisions on her own.

He sat across from her, his elbows on the table, his fingers steepled. He stared into her eyes. She tried hard not to flinch or look away.

"You have nothing to be afraid of," he said quietly.

"I want to go home," she replied.

"I'll give you a ride as soon as I clarify a few things with you."

"What things? Do I need a lawyer?"

"Why would you?"

She said nothing. She was terrified to speak, afraid he was setting a trap that she would unwittingly walk into.

"The answer is you don't. You're the victim of a crime. You're here because we need information to help us apprehend the man who hurt you." His gaze settled on the bandage an EMT had applied to her cheek. "How are you feeling?"

"Fine."

"You don't look fine," he commented, pushing away from the table and standing. "I'll be back in a minute."

He left the room.

She stayed put.

She could have walked into the hall and exited the building. She wasn't locked in. She'd checked dozens of times. Just to be certain.

But years of training were hard to break, and if Marcus was telling the truth, all the police wanted was information to help them find her would-be kidnapper. Getting him off the street was important to the well-being of the community and she couldn't let her personal fears keep her from assisting in any way she could.

Marcus returned quickly, a white mug in one hand and a package of cookies in the other. He slid both across the table before taking a seat. "You're pale. A little sugar might help."

"I'm a redhead. I'm always pale," she pointed out, lifting the mug so she would have something to do with her hands. She expected to smell coffee, but the sweet scent of chocolate and sugar drifted through the air. "Hot chocolate?"

"Seemed like a better idea than the precinct coffee. That stuff will stunt your growth." He smiled, leaning slightly away from the table, giving her plenty of space. "Officer Daniels said you were able to pick your kidnapper out of a photo lineup."

"That's right."

"We've put an APB out on the guy. Randy Warren has a lengthy rap sheet. Definitely not the kind of guy any of us would want to run into on a lonely road. I'm hoping we'll have him in custody soon. He needs to be stopped before he tries something like this again."

"Did you find the van?" She would rather think about that than the gunman wandering around town searching for another victim.

"Yes. Still off the road, the tires buried pretty deeply in mud. I think the perp tried to drive away but couldn't get enough traction to do it. We looked for footprints so we could track him. They led to the road then disappeared."

"What about the deposit? Was it there?" Her fingers were still curved around the mug, but all she could feel was the wild pounding of her heart and the sick dread in the pit of her stomach. She had taken responsibility for the deposit. If it was missing, she would have to take some of the blame.

"I'm afraid not."

"Doris is going to be upset."

"Doris is upset that you were injured. She doesn't care about the money."

"You spoke with her?"

"Yes. I called after we found the van. I want to backtrack, if you don't mind? Go over a few of the details you gave to Officer Daniels."

"That's fine." She knew how this went. She'd been through it the night her father was murdered. Even after all these years, she could remember the way the questions circled back around. Same thing presented a different way. She'd been a kid. Terrified and grief stricken. It hadn't occurred to her that she was the prime suspect until it was too late.

She was older and wiser now, and more guarded because of it.

"I mentioned that the footprints disappeared at the road. It looks like he may have been given a ride. Did you see any other vehicles on the road?"

"Actually, yes. There was another car there," she said, wishing she had thought to mention it before. It was the little details that had gotten her into trouble before. The things she'd forgotten during the first interview and remembered later. She didn't want to repeat the mistake. "An SUV. It was behind me after I left the reception hall where I made the last delivery. The driver pulled over when I ran off the road."

"Can you give me a description of the vehicle?"

She had no idea what model or make it was. Just that it was dark-colored and midsize.

"The driver did get out," she added after giving him all the details she could. "I thought he was waiting to make certain everyone was okay. Or that he might have called for help and was waiting for it to arrive."

"No calls to 9-1-1," Marcus said. "Did you get a look at the driver?"

"He was medium height. Caucasian. Medium build. That's about all I can tell you."

He nodded. "That's fine. It's more than a lot of witnesses would be able to provide. I'll assume you've been through this process before and that that's why you're nervous around law enforcement."

His comment surprised her.

It wasn't a question, but she thought he expected a response. She had no intention of explaining her nervousness. She had told the police everything she knew. Now, she wanted to leave. "If it's okay, I'd really like to go home."

"No problem. Take the cookies and hot chocolate. I'll give you a ride."

She wanted to refuse, but her vehicle was at

the bakery, her keys hanging from a hook in the office. "My truck and keys are at the bakery. It isn't far, but…"

She didn't want to walk.

Not with the man who had nearly kidnapped her still on the loose.

"I'll give you a ride. Is Doris at the bakery?"

"No. But, I've got keys." She patted her coat pocket, realized the keys were still dangling from the van's ignition. "They're in the van."

"Actually, we took them in as evidence. They've already been dusted for prints. I'll grab them, and we can get out of here." He left the room, returning just a few minutes later, keys in hand.

"Ready?"

"I was ready before I got here."

"Not too fond of police stations?"

"Is anyone?" she replied.

"Probably only people who work there." He smiled, the sharp angles of his face softening. He had been a great self-defense instructor, teaching technique and skills along with the hard-and-fast rule of avoiding dangerous situations. Crime was never the victim's fault, though some behaviors increased a person's risk of being targeted.

Kinsley avoided dangerous places. She avoided

being out late. She avoided walking through dark parking lots alone at night.

Partially because of Marcus's class. Mostly because of her experience. If she had been a clean-cut, easygoing teenager who had never dabbled in drugs or spent long nights partying with friends, she might not have been convicted of her father's murder.

She might never have been accused of it.

The real killer might have been sought and found.

That person would be in jail. Where he belonged.

Kinsley's childish mistakes had caused justice to be delayed. That haunted her. Thinking about it had kept her awake during the early years of her incarceration. The fact that she was in prison while a killer walked free had made every moment she'd spent there a hundred times worse.

Now, she was putting all her resources into finding her father's killer. He had been an FBI special agent. There were plenty of people who might have held grudges against him—criminals who wanted revenge for being tossed in jail. She was paying a PI firm thousands of dollars to go back over the case. One of the top firms in the country, it was owned by two former FBI agents and a prosecuting attorney. One of the agents was her father's former partner. Case El-wood had believed her when no one else had. He had done everything he could to help her grandparents free her.

After her exoneration, she'd hired his firm to find out the truth about what had happened. Case had sent her copies of court transcripts, evidence logs and crime scene photos. He had obtained transcripts of all the interviews conducted during the investigation. She had spent dozens of hours pouring over the files.

She was desperate for the truth, but no amount of digging seemed to uncover it.

She followed Marcus into the parking lot and to a dark blue SUV. He opened the passenger-side door and held it while she slid in.

"Just so you know…" he said before he closed the door. "Officer Daniels thought you might be withholding information when she interviewed you."

"I wasn't," she said, her pulse ratcheting up as she imagined being locked away again.

"She ran a background check," he continued.

"My past has nothing to do with this," she murmured, wishing he wasn't blocking the door. She wanted to get out and walk to her truck, because she didn't want to have this conversation with an officer of the law. She knew what they all thought. That she had been rightfully incarcerated and wrongfully exonerated. Two trials. Two different outcomes. That kind of thing left plenty of room for speculation.

"Probably not, but it would have been good to tell us about your time in prison and the circumstances of your father's death. It would have saved some time." He closed the door and walked around the vehicle.

Kinsley could have gotten out, but she was worried about what that would say about her, about the past and about her reasons for hiding it. She stayed put as he slid in behind the wheel, turned on the engine and adjusted the heat.

He didn't speak as he pulled onto the road.

She didn't, either.

But she could feel the weight of a million words waiting to be spoken. She wanted to defend herself. She wanted to tell him that she had been falsely convicted. She wanted to explain the whole thing, but explaining had gotten her into deep trouble eighteen years ago. She had learned her lesson about answering questions that hadn't been asked. This time, she was going to do herself a favor and keep her mouth shut.

In a town of just over two thousand people, it was odd to not have information about a newcomer. People talked. That was just the way it was. Someone new arrived and the neighbors gathered information like beachcombers gathering shells. They shared with other neighbors, who shared with others. Within weeks, Marcus usually knew most of what there was to know.

Kinsley had been in Frenchtown for a couple of years.

Until tonight, he'd had no idea where she had come from or why she was in Frenchtown. It hadn't been his business to find out. She hadn't caused trouble. She had lived about as quietly as anyone in small town could. Now he knew a lot more.

She had been in a Florida prison. Exonerated and released three years ago. Changed her name. Moved to Montana. In light of those things, he could understand her reluctance to be interviewed by law enforcement.

"I didn't give you that information to make you more nervous," he said.

She flinched at the sound of his voice, her tension and anxiety obvious. "Can you blame me for it?"

"No, I can't. But you've done nothing wrong. You have no reason to be afraid."

"I hadn't done anything wrong eighteen years ago, but I still ended up in prison."

"Unfortunately, miscarriages of justice happen. My officers and I do everything we can to prevent it, but sometimes we're wrong." He pulled onto Main Street, drove through the business section of town and onto the side street where Flour and Fancies had been located for as long as he could remember.

"I'm surprised you're admitting that," she said.

"Would it accomplish anything for me to deny the truth?"

"No," she responded, leaning forward as they pulled into the small parking area behind the bakery. An old Ford truck was sitting beneath the lone streetlight, the windshield and hood coated with snow and ice.

"Looks like you could use some new tires," he commented as he pulled up beside it.

"I was hoping to make it through summer."

"We aren't even through winter," he pointed out.

"In Florida, April is late spring," she replied.

"You've been here for a couple years. You've probably noticed spring doesn't come early in Montana."

"I keep hoping the first two years were a fluke and things will warm up more quickly." Her smile was strained, but she was trying to look more relaxed.

"Hope is a good thing, but it's not going to do you a lot of good when it comes to Montana winter. You're a long way from home. What brought you to Frenchtown?" he asked as he climbed out of the SUV. He'd planned to open her door, but she got out before he could.

"I needed a change. Doris was my grand-mother's best friend. She's the main reason I was finally exonerated. After my grandmother died, she took up the fight for justice." She un-locked the back door to the bakery, stepped in-side and came out moments later with another set of keys.

He waited while she relocked the door, watch-ing as snowflakes drifted onto her hair. When she turned to face him, he was surprised by the quick jump of his heart, the ratcheting up of his pulse. He had noticed her in the self-defense class mostly because she was quiet but intense, learning everything he taught quickly. He had noticed her hair, of course, but he hadn't noticed the smoothness of her skin or fear in her eyes.

He could see both now, and he wanted to tell her things would be okay. He wanted to offer comfort and support, but he didn't want to cross a line that couldn't be crossed back over again.

"Can I go now?" she asked.

"Sure," he said. He had no reason to detain her, but he was curious about her story and won-dered why she hadn't revealed it immediately.

He walked her to her the truck, waiting as she unlocked the door and climbed in.

"So, you moved here to be close to Doris?" he asked before she could close the door. "You had no other connections to the area?"

"None. But, I didn't just come to be close to her. I came to help get the business ready to sell. She's been in the red for five years. She has debt that needs to be paid, and she needs to get back in the black. A lucrative business is a good investment. If she doesn't have that, all she has is a building in a small town. Off Main Street. Not on it. It would sell eventually, but she needs funds to retire."

"I didn't realize she planned to retire."

"You don't run in the same circles as Doris," she said. She shoved the key into the ignition and turned it.

The engine sputtered and died.

She tried again with the same result. "I may need a jump start. My battery is finicky when it's cold."

"How about I give you a ride home instead? I can bring you back in the morning when the weather is clearer, and we'll jump it," he suggested.

"That seems like a lot of trouble for you."

"We're backyard neighbors, Kinsley. It's not a hardship to bring you home."

"Your backyard is acres from mine. I'd hardly call that neighbors," she pointed out.

"That's because you're from Florida. In Montana, a neighbor is whoever lives closest. Now, I don't know about you, but I'm cold, and I'd rather not stand out in this any longer if I don't have to. How about we agree you need a ride and get out of here?" He was fine, but she was still pale and now shivering.

"All right. You can give me a ride home. I'm sure Doris won't mind picking me up for church in the morning. She can bring me here after, and I'll jump it." She pulled the key and got out of the truck. She was obviously reluctant.

"If you'd rather I do it now—"

"No, it's okay. It's fine." She offered a tight smile.

"You're sure?"

"I'm sure. This makes more sense, and I'd rather not drive the truck on icy roads. Like you said, I need new tires."

"I know a place that will give you a good price. I can give you the contact information," he suggested as she climbed into his SUV.

"Thanks. I appreciate it." She wasn't enthusiastic about the offer, that was for certain.

"Or you can find someone yourself," he added as he started the engine.

She met his eyes, her tight expression easing slightly. "I'm sorry if I seem ungrateful. I'm just used to doing things on my own."

"You moved a long way to help a friend. I guess you left all your friends and family behind?"

"I left them behind when I went to prison. Aside from my grandparents and my father's fiancée, I didn't have many people who believed in me."

"What about your mother?"

"She was only in my life for a few months. She and my father were really young when they got married. My mother wasn't ready for the responsibility that came with that or with having a child."

"I'm sorry."

"Why? It has nothing to do with you."

"It doesn't, but I'm still sorry. We all need people to stand in our corners."

"It all worked out," she murmured, her arms crossed protectively.

She didn't like talking about this.

That was obvious.

But, if he were going to help her, he needed to know who she was and what she might be hiding.

He had the information he needed regarding the attempted kidnapping. And, maybe that was as simple as it seemed—someone bent on trying to make a quick buck by stealing the bakery's bank deposit.

He didn't take things at face value, though. Often, they weren't as simple as they seemed.

"I'm just trying to help you, Kinsley," he said as he pulled up in front of her bungalow.

"I know."

Maybe she did, but she seemed ready to bolt, her fingers tapping her knee, her body tense.

"Then, why are you so nervous."

"I think I explained that pretty clearly. Once you've been falsely accused of something, your naivete disappears, and you realize it could happen to anyone, and that it could happen again." She opened the door and hopped out of the SUV.

She ran up the porch stairs, shoved her keys into the lock and opened the door.

He followed. He'd been to the house a few times when he was a kid, delivering food to an elderly man who'd lived there. Aunt Winnie believed in serving the community, and she had insisted her nephew and niece do the same. After the owner had died, the property had been empty for a decade. From what he could see, Kinsley had brought it back to life. There were flowerpots hanging from the porch eaves, a small table and a wicker chair, a blue-and-white wreath hanging on the front door. Fresh paint. New windows. She might have an ancient vehicle, but the house was immaculate.

She stepped inside, pushing a code into a security pad on an interior wall near the front door. She hadn't invited him in, but he entered anyway, glancing around the brightly lit entryway. There were a few paintings on the walls. An umbrella stand near the door, a closet with its door hanging open.

She closed it and kicked her shoes off, placing them on a small shoe stand. "I'm sure I closed that door this morning."

"Does it pop open often?"

"Not since I've been here." She frowned and walked into a room to the left of the entry. He stood in the doorway, watching as she surveyed the area. An antique desk stood in the middle of the floor, a leather chair behind it. No pictures or knickknacks on the shelves of the built-in corner cabinets.

"Want me to check the house for you? Make sure no one is here?" he asked. He'd watched her unlock the door and enter the security code, but if she was worried, he'd be happy to check things out.

"I'll just check the back door. I'm sure everything is fine. The alarm was set. The doors were locked."

"Does anyone have a key and the security code?"

"Just Doris, and she'd let me know if she came by."

"Anyone else?"

"No."

"You're certain?"

"As certain as I can be." She walked through the entryway, past a staircase and into the living room. That opened into a small dining room and a set of pocket doors that led into a kitchen. She had had the place remodeled, the layout modified to be more open. The kitchen had been updated, the old 1920's stove retained, its porcelain refinished.

"You've fixed the place up," he commented as she checked the lock on the back door.

"It wasn't habitable, but Doris said it would be a perfect place once it got a makeover. She was right." She unlocked the door and then locked it again. Unlocked it. Locked it.

He touched her shoulder. "It's locked."

"I'm more worried about being able to unlock it," she said, unlocking the door one more time and stepping out onto a small back deck. A security light came on, illuminating the yard, and what looked like footprints leading away from the house.

That caught his attention. Made him pull her back.

"What?" she asked as he urged her inside.

"Probably nothing, but I want to check it out. Lock the door and stay inside." He closed the door and walked across the deck. The tracks were partially covered by fresh snow, but they were still visible. Definitely leading away and not toward the house. But anyone who'd left had to have arrived.

If the person was still around, he had some questions to ask. First, though, he had to find him.

THREE

Kinsley stared out the kitchen window, watching as Marcus made his way across the grass. Security lights illuminated the snow-covered ground and the obvious footprints that marred the nearly pristine yard. She wouldn't have noticed them. If he hadn't been with her, she'd have assumed the open closet door was a fluke.

Now, she was worried, nervous about who might have been in her house and why.

"If someone was here," she reminded herself.

She walked through the kitchen, opening the pantry closet, before stepping back into the living room. The curtains were drawn across the windows. She pulled them back. Just to be certain no one was hiding behind them.

She'd already been in the dining room and in the parlor. That left the two upstairs bedrooms and the bathroom. She checked each, pulling back curtains and opening closets. There was no one there and, as far as she could tell, nothing had been disturbed. She unlocked the basement door and walked down the steep stairs. The washer and dryer were there. Other than that, it was empty. Just a well window that she'd had installed.

She returned to the kitchen, waiting impatiently for Marcus to return. There was no way anyone could have gotten inside without setting off the alarm. She must have left the closet door open. The footprints had probably been left by a neighbor. Sometimes the teenage boys who lived one house over walked through her yard to get to their friend's house.

Kinsley wanted to believe there was nothing to her uneasiness, but she couldn't shake it. When someone knocked on the front door, she jumped.

Her heart raced as she ran to the front door and looked out the peephole. Marcus stood on the porch, hair coated with snow, flecks of it melting on his cheeks.

She let him in, her heart still beating too fast.

"Is everything okay?" she asked.

"I followed the tracks to the neighbor's property. It looks like there might have been a car parked there."

"They have a few cars and a couple of teenage boys. They walk through my yard sometimes."

"And onto your back deck?"

"I don't know. Maybe?"

"If they do, they shouldn't be. This is your private property. I can talk to their parents."

"I'd rather you not," she said quickly.

"Because?"

"I don't want to cause trouble with the neighbors." And she didn't want to call attention to herself. She liked living in relative anonymity.

"It's your choice, but if you change your mind, I'm happy to help out." He brushed melting snow from his hair, and she realized they were standing in her foyer. She should have brought him into the living room and made him some coffee.

Wasn't that what most people would do?

She had never learned all the rituals of being a good hostess. There hadn't been an opportunity for that in prison and, once released, she had spent most of her time working and trying to find her father's killer.

"Would you like some coffee?" she asked. "Or hot chocolate? I have both."

"I need to get home. My niece is probably driving my aunt crazy by now. If you need anything, let me know. I'm a quick drive or walk, and I can be here in minutes." He pulled a business card from his pocket. "Do you have a pen?"

"Sure. Right here." She hurried into the parlor and grabbed a pen from the top drawer of her desk. Her laptop computer was where she'd left it, turned off and closed, but the file folder she'd left beside it was missing. She glanced under the desk, looking for the file.

"Everything okay?" Marcus asked.

"Fine. Just misplaced something," she responded.

"You're sure?"

"I thought I left a file here, but I must have put it away."

"What kind of file?" He walked into the room, the business card still in his hand.

"Some information about the investigation into my father's murder."

"You're hoping to find the killer?"

"I'm hoping to see justice done."

She handed him the pen and he scribbled a number on the card before handing it to her. "This is my cell phone number. If anything happens, if you're uneasy or worried, call me. I'll have patrol cars ride past your house every twenty minutes, but like I said, don't hesitate to let me know if you're concerned about something."

"I appreciate that."

"I'm glad, but don't just appreciate it. Do it. You took my self-defense class. You know how important it is to listen to your gut. If you get scared, call."

"I will."

"I'll keep you updated on your case. We've issued an APB, and I'm hopeful we'll have the suspect you identified in custody before the end of the night." He walked outside and offered a quick wave before jogging to his SUV.

She closed the door and returned to the office.

The file wasn't on the desk. It wasn't in the file cabinet. She searched the house with no success. Had she taken it to work? Put it in the truck? Left it somewhere else?

She didn't remember doing any of those things, but her memory could be shoddy. Anything was possible. She just didn't think it was probable. She set the alarm, checked all the locks on the doors, rechecked every room. The house was empty. She was safe. There was no reason for her to be afraid.

But she was.

She had nearly been kidnapped. The kidnapper was still at large. Her identification had been in the glove compartment of the van. It would have been easy enough for someone to copy the information.

But why?

Because she was the sole witness to the crime he'd committed? Because she could identify him? He'd gotten the money he was after. Would he stay in town and trust the police wouldn't come after him?

She hoped not.

She hoped he had taken the money and run.

She flicked off the lights and walked up the stairs and into her bedroom. She had chosen the room at the front of the house, painting it a soft blue-gray and using bright white bed linens. Usually she slept with the door open, but she closed it and turned the key in the lock.

She set her cell phone in the charger, put Marcus's business card beside it and turned on the television to soften the hard edge of silence. After so many years of constant noise, she couldn't sleep if the house was too quiet. She thought she might get over that eventually but, for now, the low rumble of news programs was comforting. She took a quick shower and changed into flannel pajamas, ignoring the painful cuts and scrapes from her climb over the barbed-wire fence.

Her Bible was next to the bed. Well worn from two decades of early morning study, it had a faded note in the front that she read every night. Her father had written it before he had gifted her the Bible on her sixteenth birthday.

I love you, Kinsley. I am proud of you, and I know that you will find the right path and

*walk it. Wherever it leads, know that God
is with you and that my love will follow you.
Happy birthday, sweetheart.*

She hadn't been impressed with the gift when
she had received it. She'd thanked her father and
set it aside. Her grandparents had bought her a
car and her father had given her a beautiful dia-
mond and sapphire bracelet. The Bible had been
incidental and unimportant until she'd been incarcerated. Her grandparents had brought it to
her during a visit, and she had opened it a few
weeks later.

That was the first time she had seen the note
and the first time she had actually studied scrip-
ture.

Since then, reading the Bible in the morning
and reading her father's note at night had become a comforting ritual. When she finished,
she set the Bible on the bedside table and flicked
off the lamp.

She was tired. She'd gone to work at six this
morning. It was now nearly eleven. She hadn't
eaten dinner, and her stomach growled loudly,
but she didn't want to go down to the kitchen.
She kept thinking about the open closet and the
missing file. She was certain she had closed the
door and set the file next to her laptop.

Was it possible Doris had stopped by and not

bothered to mention it? She couldn't imagine that to be the case, but then, she never would have been able to imagine herself being accused and convicted of her father's murder.

Until it had happened.

After returning home from a party she had snuck out to attend and finding her father's lifeless body, the last thing she had been thinking about was making sure she said and did the right things. It hadn't occurred to her that she was a suspect. She had been too young to realize she needed to protect herself from the police. She had walked into the police precinct hoping and praying that her father was still alive.

She had answered every question.

She had been honest and open, her grief and terror pouring out as she had answered question after question.

She had been a fifteen-year-old kid who had never been violent, never given anyone any reason to suspect she would murder someone. Less than twenty-four hours later, she had been arrested. A year after that, she had been tried and convicted of first degree murder.

Now, she understood that anything was possible.

She would call Doris in the morning and ask. If Doris had been there, Kinsley would have peace of mind. If she hadn't, it was time to change the locks and the security code.

She closed her eyes, listening to the muted sound of the television and the quiet swish of wind beneath the eaves. Marcus had said they were looking for the man who had tried to kidnap her. He had told her patrol cars would be driving by her place throughout the night. She needed to trust the system to do what it was designed to do.

But her trust had been irreparably broken. She wasn't a naive teenager who believed the truth would always prevail. She was nearly thirty-four. Old enough to understand that good didn't always win. If her father, Michael King's murder hadn't proven that, her conviction of the crime would have.

She wanted to call Elizabeth Harvey. Before the world had gone haywire, Elizabeth had been her father's fiancée. Bright, charismatic and brilliant, Elizabeth had been a prosecuting attorney for the state of Florida when Kinsley had been arrested. Now she was a senator, her name a front-runner for candidacy in the next presidential election. She was married now, had a couple of kids, but she still kept in contact with Kinsley. She had been at the prison when Kinsley was released. She'd allowed her to stay in one of the rental properties she and her real-estate mogul husband owned. When Kinsley had mentioned that Doris might need help, Elizabeth had encouraged her to go.

Elizabeth would talk her down from her fear. She would convince her that she had nothing to worry about. She had been the calm voice of reason during the worst moments of Kinsley's life.

She would be the voice of reason again, but Kinsley didn't want to wake her. Elizabeth had moved forward with her life. She had a wonderful family and great career. She didn't need to be pulled into the drama that always seemed to surround Kinsley.

She forced herself to relax, concentrating on her breathing and on the hushed sound of the television until she drifted off to sleep.

Kinsley didn't know what woke her.

She had no idea what time it was.

She only knew that she was awake, staring into the darkness. The television was off, the house eerily silent. Had the electricity gone out? She reached for the bedside lamp, freezing as the quiet creak of the stair treads drifted into her room.

Terrified, she grabbed her phone and Marcus's business card. She dialed his number with shaky fingers. He answered quickly.

"Hello? Kinsley? Is everything okay?"

"I think someone is in the house," she whispered.

"I'm on my way."

Just like that.

No other questions.

He was coming, and she should feel better. She should be convincing herself that she had imagined the creak, that the electricity had gone out for some reason other than an intruder.

She stayed still, the phone clutched in her hand.

Listening.

Was that another creak? The soft rustle of fabric?

Was someone outside the door?

She eased out of bed, crept across the room and pressed her ear to the wood. Nothing. Just the quiet rush of her pulse in her ears. She touched the key, ready to unlock the door and look out into the hall. Somewhere in the house a door closed, the quiet thud making her jump.

She bit back a scream and moved away from the door. She had knives in the kitchen but no weapons in her room. She hadn't imagined she would ever need one.

Another soft thud.

Another door closing?

She wasn't sure.

She wanted to call Marcus again. To make

sure that help was on the way and, maybe, to not feel so alone.

The house had gone silent.

No more thuds or creaks.

But, something was off. She could feel it the same way she could feel her heart beating behind her ribs.

She waited what seemed like hours. Heard a soft pop and a quiet hiss, caught the unmistakable smell of smoke.

A fire?

Was the house on fire?

She touched doorknob. It felt cool.

She had fire alarms with new batteries.

If there was a fire, one of them should be going off.

She flicked the light switch. Nothing. No lights. No sounds except that quiet hiss and pop. The smell of smoke grew stronger. The house was definitely on fire! She pressed her hand against the door. No heat, but she didn't dare open the door. The intruder might be waiting in the hall.

She ran for the window. If the only way out of the house was a two-story drop, she'd drop two stories. No way had she survived prison and an attempted kidnapping to die in a house fire.

She wrenched open the window, climbed onto the windowsill, her legs dangling over the edge.

It was a far drop to the ground. Jumping wasn't a good option.

She turned, easing over the edge on her stomach, smoke billowing into the room and drifting out the window.

She coughed, her body slipping, her fingers scrambling for a hold. She needed to drop. She knew she did, but she couldn't make herself do it. The fire wasn't an accident. Someone had been in the house. That same person could be waiting below.

Who?

Why?

She kept to herself. She didn't cause trouble. She went about her life in the quietest way possible. No one should want to harm her. Unless it was someone from her past.

Her father's killer, trying to keep her from finding the truth? After all these years, had she woken a sleeping monster?

"Kinsley!" someone shouted. "Let go! I'll catch you!"

She glanced down, saw Marcus. He was just below, arms held out as if he could catch her.

"I don't want to hurt you," she yelled, her feet scraping the siding as she tried to keep from dropping. "Move out of the way."

"Let go!" he repeated.

More smoke billowed out, the acrid scent

burning the back of her throat. She coughed, her fingers slipping, her feet losing traction. She tried to pull up but couldn't hold on. Her fingers slid over smooth wood and she fell.

Marcus barely managed to catch Kinsley before she hit the ground. His hands clasped her waist, his fingers digging into her side. He set her down, holding on as she caught her balance.

"You got here fast," she said as she swung to face him.

"I ran through the fields. It seemed faster than getting in the car and driving. Are you okay?" he asked as he led her away from the house. Flames were shooting out a first-floor window, licking their way up the wood siding.

"I'm fine," she said, her focus on the house. "But my house…"

"I called for fire crews as soon as I saw the flames. They'll be able to extinguish that in no time." He hoped. He had no idea the extent of the blaze, but he had seen it as he'd crossed the acres of field that separated their property. "What happened?" he asked.

"I don't know. I was asleep and then I wasn't. I thought I heard someone on the stairs. Then, I heard the fire and smelled smoke. I was worried the intruder might be waiting for me, so I decided to go out the window."

"Good decision," he responded, but his mind was jumping ahead, putting pieces of this newest puzzle together. The guy who'd stolen the deposit hadn't been apprehended. He had a lot to gain if Kinsley died.

That was the easy route to take.

But, she was pursuing justice for her father. That might be making someone nervous.

"Are you sure Doris is the only one with the security code?" he asked.

"Yes, and she would never hurt me."

He wasn't going to argue that. Doris had been a law-abiding citizen for longer than either of them had been alive.

"You're sure you turned it on?"

"I think you witnessed how careful I am about locks," she replied. "But my electricity was off when I woke up. Would that take out the security system?"

"Off?"

"Yes. I sleep with the TV on. When I woke, it was off. The lights weren't working." She shuddered.

He patted her shoulder.

He wasn't the best at giving comfort.

He knew that.

He'd been special ops in the military. He knew how to defend and protect people he cared about, but he had no idea how to offer them comfort during tough times. "It's going to be okay," he said.

The words sounded lame.

They *were* lame.

A go-to when a person didn't know what else to say.

"As long as I'm not carted away and locked in jail for the next fifteen years for a crime I didn't commit, they probably will be." She offered a tense smile and brushed a thick strand of hair from her cheek. "Do you think this is because of what happened earlier? Maybe an attempt to keep me from being a witness?"

"That would be my first guess."

"What would be your second?"

"Something to do with your father's murder."

"My father was murdered a long time ago, Marcus."

"And, you digging into what happened may be making someone very uncomfortable." He shrugged out of his coat and dropped it around her shoulders. "How about we go back to my place? We can wait there until the fire crew is finished."

"They haven't arrived," she pointed out, her focus still on the house and the flames shooting out the window.

"Kinsley, it's not going to make you feel any better to watch the house burn," he said quietly.

"I know, but it's my place. I don't feel like I can leave."

He understood that. He would have felt the same, but it was cold and she wasn't dressed for the weather, her bare feet peeking out from beneath the cuffs of her flannel pajamas. "Your feet are going to freeze."

"Not possible," she murmured.

"In this kind of weather? Trust me, it is."

"Not possible because they're already frozen," she explained, limping around the back of the house and opening a combination lock on a shed. The door swung open and she disappeared inside.

For a moment, he thought she might be planning to stay there.

Then she reappeared, wearing a down parka and snow boots. She held out his coat. "Better put this back on."

"You keep spare winter gear in your shed?"

"When I first moved here, I had a fear of locking myself out in the cold."

"The locks on old doors can be tricky," he agreed as he put his coat on.

"I wasn't used to carrying a key around. I was worried I'd forget it. I still worry. But not as much. I can hear the firetrucks. I really hope they can put this out before it does more damage."

She headed around the side of the house.

Marcus followed, stopping short when he heard fabric rustling. He glanced around, looking for signs that they weren't alone. Kinsley's yard was well kept. A couple of fruit trees. A small garden plot. Shrubs to the left that separated her property from the neighbor's.

Was that where the sound had come from?

"What's wrong?" she asked, heading back in his direction.

He heard the soft click of a gun safety being removed and knew what was about to happen.

He shouted for Kinsley to get down and threw himself in her direction as the first shot exploded. He landed on top of her, covering her body with his as a bullet slammed into the ground nearby.

He pulled his firearm, aiming toward the shrubs. "Police! Put your weapon down!"

There was a flurry of movement and then silence.

"Chief! Is everything okay?" Charlotte Daniels ran around the side of the house, firearm drawn. "I was running patrol past the house, saw the fire and then I heard gunfire."

"Someone shot at Kinsley. Stay here. I'm going to find out who it was."

He didn't wait for her response.

The perp already had a head start. Marcus

was going to make certain he didn't get more of one. Kinsley had been attacked twice in one night. Her house had been set on fire while she was in it.

Was Randy Warren trying to silence her? His rap sheet was impressive. He had a lengthy arrest record in Missoula where he was a known drug user and supplier. He had an assault-and-battery charge, which was later dropped and petty theft offences. He'd been out of jail for three months after serving ten years for a domestic violence conviction. Had he fallen back into old habits?

Marcus needed to find him.

He needed to stop him.

And he needed to make certain he wouldn't have a chance to come after Kinsley again.

FOUR

By the time the fire was out and the fire crews had cleared the area, the sun was rising. Kinsley stood in the driveway, watching as the fire investigator walked out the front door and down the porch steps. She knew what he was going to say. She was prepared for it.

"Arson," he explained as he approached.

"I figured that," she replied. On the outside, she might look like she was okay. Inside, she was shaking like a leaf, wondering how her life had come to this.

Hadn't she been through enough?

Fifteen years in prison for a crime she hadn't committed, losing all her friends and some of her relatives, realizing that exoneration by a jury didn't mean exoneration in the court of public opinion.

Wasn't that enough?

"You were inside the house when the fire was

set, right?" he asked, jotting notes rather than meeting her eyes.

"That's correct."

"Tell me about your fire alarms."

"What do you mean?" she asked, surprised and thrown off balance by the question.

"When did you replace the batteries?"

"January first. Just like always."

"There were no batteries in any of them," the investigator said, finally looking up from his notebook.

"No batteries?" she repeated.

"That's correct. If you hadn't heard the intruder, you may not have woken up in time to escape." He spoke matter-of-factly, as if this sort of thing happened every day.

Maybe it did, but it had never happened to her.

"Why would someone take the batteries out of my fire alarms?" she asked, knowing he had no answers.

"That's what I was going to ask you. Do you have any enemies? Anyone who might want to harm you?"

"Probably," she responded truthfully.

That got his attention.

He met her eyes. "The police are going to want to know who. It's my job to figure out whether a fire is accidental. They get to figure out who set it."

"I understand."

"You also understand that any insurance payout will be held until you are able to prove you aren't responsible?"

"Why would I set fire to my house?" she asked, shocked by the thought more than by his comment.

"Money? That's a powerful motivator. Ninety-five percent of our arson cases can be traced back to it. People want to offload property for profit." He shrugged, his gaze shifting to a group of police officers. "Not that I'm accusing you of anything. I'm here to collect facts, to decide if a fire is arson or accident. It looks like the chief is back. I'm going to fill him in. Wait here."

He walked toward the group of police officers now crossing the front yard.

Kinsley followed. She had stopped blindly obeying orders the day she'd walked out of prison.

Marcus was standing at the front of the group, his wool coat open to reveal flannel pajama bottoms and a black T-shirt. The cuffs of his pajama pants were tucked halfway into snow boots. He'd obviously left his house without dressing for the weather. Something she hadn't noticed before.

"Is it okay to enter the house?" Marcus asked the fire investigator.

"Depends on how worried you are about contaminating evidence."

"I'm worried about it, but Kinsley lives in the house. Her DNA and fingerprints are all over it. I don't see any harm in her going inside. As long as it's safe."

"It's safe. The fire was small. Mostly confined to what looks to be an office on the main level. Definitely arson."

"You collected what you need?" Marcus asked as he walked to the front door.

"I did."

"There's no sign of forced entry here or at the back door. No broken windows." Marcus opened the door and gestured for Kinsley to enter.

She stepped inside, the sharp, thick, scent of smoke seeming to wrap around her chest. She took a deep breath. Just to be certain she could. The electricity was off, but she didn't need lights to find the coat closet and grab her purse, which she'd hung inside the closet.

"Need some light?" Marcus asked.

"I'm good."

Her cell phone was upstairs, abandoned somewhere in her room. The door was locked, but there was a set of spare keys in a kitchen drawer.

She headed in that direction.

Marcus grabbed the back of her parka before she could go more than a couple of steps. "Where are you going?"

"To get a key to my bedroom. I want to get my cell phone."

"I'll have someone do that. For now, you can borrow mine if you need one." He was heading back outside, tugging her along with him.

She didn't bother protesting.

The sooner the evidence team processed the scene, the sooner she could start cleaning up. It was going to take more than a broom, a mop and some furniture polish to make the place habitable again. She'd have to hire a company to do the work, because she wanted it done right. When she'd moved to Montana, she hadn't planned to stay long. Just a year or two. Enough time for Doris to put things in order and get Flour and Fancies sold.

And that was taking longer than she had anticipated.

Kinsley'd had no idea just how poorly the business had been doing. Despite a strong local following, sales had declined during the last decade. As Doris had aged, the bakery had done the same. The place had needed painting and updating. The antiquated kitchen had needed an overhaul.

Kinsley had designed a five-year plan for building the business and getting it sold. They were two and a half years in and ahead of schedule. The bakery was already in the black. They'd expanded their delivery area, created a website to allow for online orders, and begun advertising in regional newspapers.

But Kinsley had promised five years.

She needed a house to live in while she fulfilled that promise. She didn't want to buy another one. She didn't want to wait months while this one was put to right.

"It's going to be okay. Once the scene is processed, you can get a team in here to start cleaning up," Marcus said as if reading her mind.

"I'll need to stay in a hotel while they're working. The place looked waterlogged and it already reeked. A few days of wet wallboard and I'll have all kinds of mold and mildew problems."

"There are several companies in Missoula that do fire and water cleanup. I'm sure Bill can give you a recommendation."

"Bill thinks I started the fire myself. To get some kind of insurance payout," she muttered.

She immediately wished the words back. The last thing she wanted to do was to call attention to herself as a possible suspect in the arson.

Marcus stopped walking, swinging around to face her. They were a few yards from Bill,

Charlotte and the other deputy, so he kept his voice low so his words wouldn't carry. "Did he say that?"

"Not in so many words."

"Good, because it's not his job to decide who the arsonist is."

"It's not me," she said quickly, her voice louder than intended.

"The idea hadn't even crossed my mind."

"But now it has?"

"You weren't alone in the house, Kinsley. I found a trail of footprints leading from your cellar door to the neighbor's driveway. There were tire marks there."

"Did you talk to the neighbors? Maybe they saw something?"

"I did. They were sound asleep, and the tracks stopped at a bend in their driveway. There was no way they could have seen the vehicle from their house, but the property across the street has a doorbell camera. They caught video of a vehicle pulling into the driveway."

"You saw it?"

"Yes."

"Did you get a license plate number?"

"The image wasn't clear enough, but I did see the vehicle. It was a black Toyota SUV. I've already sent the video to the crime lab. They may be able to clean up the image and get us an exact make and model."

"You think it's the vehicle I saw earlier, don't you?" she asked, the image of the SUV and the man standing near it flitting through her mind.

"It makes more sense than another random crime with the same victim. Frenchtown's crime rate is low. The kinds of problems we have are usually petty theft, breaking and entering, drugs. To have two violent crimes in one night is very unusual. The fact that you were the victim both times? It's inconceivable that the crimes aren't related."

"Bill said there were no batteries in my smoke alarms," she said. "And there were footprints on my back deck earlier. Do you think the person who tried to kidnap me came here to set this up?" She waved at the house.

"Currently, I think just about anything is possible," he responded. "Let's go see what else Bill has to say. Maybe he has some insight that will help the investigation."

He touched her shoulder, his palm resting there as he steered her toward the officers and the fire investigator.

In other circumstances, she would have pulled away.

After so many years of prison life, she didn't like people in her space. She didn't like being touched. She certainly didn't want a police officer anywhere near her.

But there was something comforting about Marcus.

Something calming.

When they reached the group and his hand fell away, she was almost sorry.

Almost?

She was sorry. Being alone had its perks, but it also had its challenges. She might not have anyone depending on her, she might not have to worry about disappointing or hurting anyone, but she also didn't have anyone to lean on when things got tough.

That was a fact she had accepted long ago.

It wasn't one she wanted to change, but that didn't mean she couldn't appreciate the comfort of having someone in her corner. She could appreciate it. She wasn't looking for it, though. Especially not from a law enforcement officer.

Kinsley knew the value of men and women in uniform, but her knee-jerk reaction was to stay as far away as possible. Even now, even knowing that Marcus was on her side, she was nervous. One wrong word, one unexpected and unusual reaction, and she could go from being a victim to being a suspect.

She wouldn't let that happen again.

She had spent enough time in prison. She had

no intention of going back. She took a few steps away, ignoring Marcus's questioning look. He knew her past. He could understand her reaction to being surrounded by law enforcement or not. It didn't matter to her.

What did matter was finding the person who had tried to kidnap her. The person who had set fire to her house. The person who seemed determined to hurt her.

Kinsley's discomfort was obvious.

She stood a few feet away, wrapped in a down parka that looked to be three sizes too large, her attention jumping from one person to another as the fire investigator went over his findings. Charlotte had been first on the scene. She would be the lead. Jett Bryant and Sam Gordon were also there. Jett had seniority. He'd been with the Frenchtown police for nearly two decades. A widower with teenage twins, he'd was devoted to the job, but his kids always came first.

That was something Marcus was learning to do—prioritize family. Until Rosemarlyn's arrival, his job had been his family. He'd been completely devoted to it.

"So, you're saying this was a sloppy attempt at arson?" Jett asked, his arms crossed, his gun belt squeaking slightly as he shifted weight from one foot to the other.

"I'm saying it was arson. I'm saying the fire didn't spread upstairs as intended because there wasn't enough accelerant. If you want to call that a sloppy arson attempt, you're welcome to, but it won't be in my report." The fire investigator glanced at his notes. "The curtains in the office did catch fire, but that was due to proximity. There was no accelerant on or around the windows. Most of it was on the desk and the file cabinet beside it."

"The desk and file cabinet?" Kinsley repeated. Her skin was parchment pale, her freckles obvious even in the dim light.

The fire investigator glanced at his notes again and nodded. "Desk. File cabinet. There was a liberal amount of accelerant on the area rug. Just a line of it running from there into the foyer. The fire burned itself out, though. The wood floor didn't catch easily or quickly. You'll need to get an expert in to assess the damages, but we've already discussed that." He pulled business cards from his wallet and passed them out. "I'll forward a copy of my report to the police department and to you, Ms. Garrett. You'll need it for insurance purposes."

"Thank you," Kinsley murmured, tucking the card into her coat pocket.

Marcus didn't think she planned to look at it again.

Hopefully, she had good insurance on the house. From what he'd seen when he'd walked her inside, there was more water than fire damage, but the place smelled of smoke. As she'd mentioned: couple of days without cleaning and mildew and mold would start growing.

"No need for thanks. I'm just doing what I'm paid to do."

"Any idea when we'll have the report?" Charlotte asked.

"I try to finish the day I complete the inspection, but I give twenty-four to thirty-six hours as a guideline, and I don't make any promises. If there's another suspicious fire, and I get called to it, things might take longer. You have my information. If it isn't in your hands in a reasonable amount of time, send an email or give me a call."

"Thank you," Charlotte said.

He nodded, closed his notebook and walked away.

Kinsley seemed determined to do the same. She dug into her purse, pulled out keys and then sighed. "I forgot, my truck is still at Flour and Fancies."

"Are you planning to go somewhere?" Jett asked, his expression hidden by a shadow.

"I can't stay here for the night," Kinsley pointed out. "Officer Daniels took my statement earlier. Unless you needed something else from me, I thought I'd check into a hotel."

"There aren't a lot of options in Frenchtown. Are you thinking the extended stay or the bed-and-breakfast on Main Street?" Marcus asked.

"I hadn't thought about it." Kinsley eyed the façade of the house. It didn't look damaged. Aside from the acrid scent that hung in the air, there was very little external evidence of the fire.

"Just looking at it from here, I'd like to think that I'd only need to be in hotel for a couple days, but the inside is going to need significant work." She sighed again. "I guess the extended stay. I'll call Doris and ask her to give me a ride to the bakery. It's early, but she usually makes doughnuts for church. I'm sure she'll be awake." She frowned. "I still need my cell phone."

"You can use mine," Marcus offered. He'd allowed her into the entryway but didn't want her anywhere else in the house until the evidence was collected.

"It's okay. I can wait."

"Out here?"

"I don't currently have anywhere else to go," she responded. "If you hadn't noticed, my house is a mess, and I can't go inside."

"I can take you to my place," he offered.

She met his eyes. "You're place?"

"We're neighbors. That seems like a neighborly thing to do—offer you a place to stay warm while you wait."

"I think it's best if I stay here," Kinsley said. "Someone has tried to kill me twice tonight. I would hate to have it happen again while I was with your family."

She had a point.

One Marcus hadn't thought about because he still wasn't used to putting his family ahead of his job.

He wasn't used to having a family.

Not one that relied on him.

Charlotte walked toward them, her expression hard. "It would probably be best if you got out of the way for a while, Kinsley. No offense, but there is a lot going on here, and it may be a while before you can get back inside."

"We were just discussing that," Marcus said.

"I have an apartment above my garage. It's an efficiency. A pull-out couch. Small kitchen area. Bathroom. Not anything to write home about, but it's within walking distance of the bakery, and it's empty. How about you take her there?" Charlotte said.

"How about I be included in this conversation?" Kinsley muttered.

"I'm not trying to exclude you. Just trying to expedite things," Charlotte replied. "You're going to need a place to stay while this place is cleaned up. My apartment is sitting there empty. Why not use it?"

"I couldn't put you out like that," Kinsley protested.

"You wouldn't be." Charlotte's gaze shifted to the driveway. A white Fire Marshall's van was turning in from the road. She dug into her pocket and pulled out a keychain. She removed one key and handed it to Kinsley. "Here's the key. Marcus knows where I live. He can give you a lift."

"I really can't…" Kinsley began, but Charlotte was rushing toward the van.

"You may as well take her up on the offer," Marcus said.

"I don't like to inconvenience anyone," Kinsley murmured, her focus on the key.

"How is it an inconvenience if she offered?" Marcus asked.

"We don't even know each other."

"And you won't need to get to know each other, if you don't want to. She has an empty apartment. You need a place to stay. It seems like a God-thing to me," he said, hoping to convince her. He'd been to Charlotte's house many times. She lived on an acre of land right in the center of town. Not only was the house surrounded by other properties, but the police station was four blocks away. The garage was behind the house—a detached, two-story building that Charlotte's brother had lived in while going to college. It was easily visible from the street and from neighboring properties. An improvement over Kinsley's current location.

"A God-thing?" she asked, raising a dark red brow.

"He has ways of working things out for us. If we let him, but if you're uncomfortable because Charlotte is a police officer, I understand."

"It's not because she's a police officer," Kinsley muttered. "I'd feel the same way if anyone offered me a place to stay."

"What way is that?"

"Like a charity case. I'm not. I can afford a hotel, so that seems like a better solution."

"The hotel is right off the main highway, Kinsley," Marcus pointed out. "Easy access for anyone who wants to make a quick getaway."

"Are you implying that I won't be safe there?"

"I'm not implying. I'm pointing out that you'll be safer in a location that is closer to the police and closer to a police officer."

She frowned, tucking a thick strand of hair behind her ear. "I guess I can hang out there until she finishes her shift. Once I have my cell phone, I can make other plans."

"I'll take you there. We'll have to get my SUV

and, if you don't mind waiting a few minutes, I'll change before I drive into town."

"You don't think the citizens of Frenchtown are going to appreciate seeing their police chief walking around in his pajamas?" Kinsley asked, a hint of amusement in her eyes.

"They might appreciate it, but I won't appreciate hearing about it for the next forty years of my life," he responded.

She chuckled, the soft sound taking him by surprise.

He hadn't thought she had it in her. Not on a night when she had been through so much. Not when he knew her background, where she had been, how far she had come to get away from the dregs of her past.

Kinsley had every right to be tense and defensive around the police. She had every right to be upset about the intruder who had breached the sanctuary of her home.

Despite those things, she was able to laugh.

He liked that.

If he gave himself some time, he would probably discover a lot of things to like about Kinsley. Right now, though, the only thing he wanted to discover was the location of the person who had tried to kill her.

FIVE

A lot could change in two days.

Late winter weather could turn mild.

Snow and ice could melt.

Anonymity could become notoriety.

And a bakery that was generally empty on Monday afternoon could be filled with customers.

Kinsley scooped pumpkin muffin batter into a tin and tried to ignore the din drifting in from the service area. Flour and Fancies wasn't large. Just a few small tables. Two chairs at each. Two booths huddled next to the windows that looked out onto Main Street. Before Kinsley's arrival, the vast majority of business had been done Friday and Saturday. Monday mornings had also been lucrative. People had stopped for a dozen doughnuts or a box of scones to take to the office. By midmorning, though, winter weekdays had been dead.

Business had steadily increased the last couple of years.

But it was never this good.

Kinsley slid the muffins into the oven, set the timer and started assembling the ingredients for Doris's blueberry scones. Baking wasn't Kinsley's thing; she had learned to cook in the prison kitchen. Not the kind of fancy baked goods that Doris produced, but she had learned how to follow a recipe. She hadn't planned to help in the bakery but, financially, it had made sense. She didn't need an income. She'd received reparation from the state for the time she had spent in prison. Her father's estate had been saved in trust for her, and her grandparents had also left her money. Financially, she was set. She could afford to help out as a favor to the woman whose determined efforts had helped free her from prison.

At first, she had made simple things—cookies, scones, pound cakes. Doris had watched carefully the first few months and then she had announced that Kinsley had the gift.

Whatever that meant, it had translated into Kinsley learning how to bake and decorate complicated cakes and pastries. Most days she found working in the kitchen soothing. She'd spent the early morning hours prepping dough and getting things ready for the breakfast rush. She'd run deliveries in the early afternoon and then close up the shop in the evening.

Currently, there was nothing soothing about the kitchen.

Voices carried through the narrow hall that led from the front of the house to the kitchen. Male, female, young, old. They all seemed to have crammed into the small serving area, hoping to get information on what had happened to Kinsley.

She wasn't talking.

She had made that clear when a reporter had showed up at Charlotte's house hoping for the scoop. She still hadn't been granted access to her house, and she'd had to buy clothes, toiletries and groceries. She'd been hauling her purchases up the stairs when a reporter had rounded the side of Charlotte's house. Kinsley had no idea who had given away her location, but she'd been very quick to send the reporter packing.

She'd do the same if they showed up at the bakery, but she couldn't send all the nosy customers away. As long as they purchased something, they had every right to be there, and a few strong sales days was going to be good for Doris.

"So, buck up and stop moping about the attention," she muttered, taking chilled dough out of the fridge and cutting it into triangles. The scent of vanilla bean and orange zest drifted from the baking sheet. Her stomach growled in response. She hadn't eaten breakfast. She glanced at the clock. She hadn't eaten lunch, either. It was nearly 4:00 p.m. Past her normal break time. By this time of day, she was usually thinking about closing down the kitchen and closing up the shop.

Instead, she was shoving another pan of scones into one of the ovens and praying that Ryker Patterson wasn't breaking any land-speed records while making deliveries. Ryker worked front-of-the-house a few days a week. A college freshman, he had no intention of sticking around Frenchtown after he graduated. For now, he commuted to Missoula to attend a community college while he saved money to move to Seattle. He had a good head on his shoulders and good interpersonal skills. He communicated well with customers, worked hard and got whatever job he was assigned done.

But he drove fast.

The bakery had received several complaints about the van speeding through town. His delivery privileges had been revoked, but today wasn't a typical day. The bakery needed all hands on deck.

Doris and Madeline Rothchild were working

the front of the house. A single mother, Madeline worked two jobs to provide for her daughter. She moved fast, talked faster and never seemed to stop. Kinsley was working in the kitchen. That left Ryker to make deliveries in his Chevy Blazer. The bakery's van had been impounded for evidence. As far as Kinsley knew, the police hadn't given a time frame for its return. Her truck still needed to be jump-started. Not that she had any intention of lending the vehicle to Ryker.

Madeline rushed into the kitchen, her short hair covered by a snood, her blue-framed glasses hanging from a chain around her neck. She hurried into the walk-in cooler and rolled out a rack of muffins. "How's it going back here, Kinsley?"

"I'm doing fine. I've got the last batch of scones in the oven," Kinsley responded.

"Good. I'll take over for you in here, if you can take these up to the front of the house."

"You prefer working up front, and I don't mind spending my day in the kitchen."

"Sorry. I should have clarified. The police want to talk to you. They're in the service area, gumming up the works. So to speak. Doris sent me to get you."

"They want to talk to me?"

"That is what they said."

"About what?"

"Honey, they didn't give me the 4-1-1. They just asked to speak with you. But, if I were you, I wouldn't complain. Not if Chief Hot Stuff was wanting to speak with me." She smirked, her black eyes glinting with humor.

"You're twenty-seven, Madeline."

"And?"

"He must be closing in on forty." Kinsley washed her hands, dried them on her apron and resisted the urge to take off her hair net. She didn't care how she looked. Or, she shouldn't care. All that mattered was finding out why the police wanted to speak with her.

"And?" Madeline repeated, arching a perfectly shaped brow. She was a beautiful young woman whose ex-husband had left her while she was pregnant. Now she had a three-year-old daughter and two jobs. Somehow, she still managed to be cheerful and upbeat.

"Don't you think someone closer to your age might be better dating material?"

"I'm not looking for a date. I'm looking for a guy who is mature enough to appreciate the responsibilities that come with being a parent." Some of the good humor slipped from her face. "And, to be honest, that's hard to find in guys my age, but Chief Hot Stuff isn't here to see me. You'd better head out there. He and Officer Daniels look pretty serious."

Kinsley hurried into the service area, stopping next to Doris, who stood in front of the cash register, her salt-and-pepper curls springing as she taped one of the white bakery boxes shut. "Here you are, dear. Six blueberry scones. I threw in an extra for your aunt Helen." She handed the box to a slim woman who was so busy gawking at Kinsley that she barely managed to keep it from falling to the floor.

"I heard the police are here," Kinsley said quietly to Doris as she scanned the crowd.

"I sent them outside. Too much commotion in here to try to have a conversation. Plus, I'm trying to keep the line moving." Doris looked tired, her skin pale, her usual cheerful expression strained.

"I'll go talk to them. I'll be as quick as I can."

"You've been here since four thirty this morning without a break. Take as long as you need. The crowd is dying down, and we'll be putting out the Closed sign in a few minutes." She glanced at the clock that hung over the entrance. "I should have done it twenty minutes ago, but I hate to disappoint people."

"I'll flip it on my way out," Kinsley said. "And, I'll come back as soon as I can to help close the shop and prep for tomorrow." She

stepped around the counter, the customers part-
ing as she moved. Most people in town knew
very little about her. That was the way she liked
it. Though she didn't like the awkward silence
that settled over the crowd as she passed. If she
were friends with the people there, they'd have
called out her name, asked how she was, maybe
tried to console her because of what she'd been
through.

Instead, they said nothing, just watched as she
flipped the sign to Closed and walked outside.

Marcus and Charlotte were standing a few
yards away, talking quietly as they waited. She
bypassed a few people still hoping to get into
the bakery and walked toward the officers, the
evening sun filtering through a thin cloud layer,
the early spring air redolent with the scent of
freshly cut grass. If it had been any other day,
she would have inhaled deeply and enjoyed the
sweet smell, but she was nervous, her stomach
churning, her thoughts racing.

Had they discovered something that incrimi-
nated her?

Kinsley'd spent the previous day and night
thinking about the fire investigator's veiled accusations. She'd worried about calling her insurance company, because she'd been terrified that
doing it too soon would make her look guilty.

"Kinsley, it's good to see you again," Marcus

said, his warm smile almost enough to distract her from her worries. Almost enough to disarm her into thinking this was just a follow-up visit and that he and Charlotte weren't fishing for information that might point the investigation in her direction.

"It's good to see you, too," she mumbled, offering a quick handshake to both of them. "Is everything okay?"

"We have a few more questions to ask," he responded.

"About?"

"How about we walk over to the station? We'll have more privacy there." He glanced at the line of people still standing near the bakery door. Most were trying to sneak glances in their direction. A few were out-and-out staring.

"That's fine," she responded. Not because she wanted to go to the police station but because she didn't want to have a conversation in front of an audience.

"If you'd rather wait until the bakery closes, that's not a problem," Marcus offered, glancing at the line again.

"It was closing time twenty minutes ago. It was so busy Doris didn't turn the sign." She tried to make small talk, keep her tone light, not act as nervous as she felt.

"Looks like you were working in the kitchen today," Charlotte said, her focus on Kinsley's head.

"I thought I'd be too distracting if I were in the front of the house."

"The town does seem to be buzzing about what happened this weekend. You probably don't want them to talk about how we made you leave the bakery so suddenly you didn't even have time to take off your hair net," she replied, not unkindly.

"My hair net... Right. Thanks." Kinsley snagged it off, shoved it in her apron pocket and tried to ignore the hot flush of embarrassment staining her cheeks.

She had done nothing wrong.

She had no reason to be nervous.

She had no reason to apologize.

No reason to hide.

They reached the end of the block where Main Street bisected a county road. A streetlight signaled that it was safe to cross, and she stepped off the curb a few feet ahead of Charlotte and Marcus. She knew she couldn't avoid them, but she would rather not have everyone in town talking about how she had been escorted to the police station.

Tires squealed as she hit the midway point of the road. Surprised, she glanced in the direction of the sound, seeing a car barreling toward her.

Someone screamed. Marcus shouted. She tried to jump out of the way, but the car switched direction, the driver seeming to steer the vehicle straight at her.

Marcus grabbed Kinsley's shirt and yanked her back. She stumbled, falling into him as the car sped past. Charlotte sprinted across the street, not bothering to say a word. He knew she was running for her squad car, hoping to catch the careless driver.

If it was a careless driver.

It seemed as if the car had been aiming straight for Kinsley.

"Are you okay?" Marcus asked, his arm wrapped around Kinsley's waist.

"I'm fine," she responded, breaking contact quickly. Moving away and putting distance between them.

Her cheeks were pink, her eyes the darkest blue he had cver sccn. She had freckles on her cheeks and a few on her forehead, covered by heavy bangs that had fallen in her face when she'd removed the hairnet.

"That was a little too close for comfort." He tracked the car as it sped around a corner and out of sight. Bright blue Honda Civic. No visible license plates. He hadn't gotten a look at the driver, but he thought he knew who it might be.

Randy Warren still hadn't been apprehended.

Despite the dragnet they'd set, despite having every one of his known associates under surveillance, somehow Warren continued to move under the radar.

"I don't understand what's going on." She blew the bangs from her eyes and tucked a loose strand of hair back into her tight bun. There was flour on her apron and sprinkled across the front of her dark blue shirt.

"Our theory is that Randy Warren is trying to silence you," he responded, cupping her elbow and urging her the rest of the way across the street.

"Why would he want to do that? You've said he has a lengthy criminal record. It's not like he hasn't been in trouble with the law before."

"We've thought about that."

"And?"

"We don't have an answer. That's why we want to talk to him. He's the only one who knows why he's doing what he's doing."

"Assuming it's him."

"Who else could it be?" Marcus asked, curious to hear her answer. Previously, she had claimed to have no enemies. Was she changing her story?

"I don't know," she murmured, her gaze shifting away.

She had an idea.

He was certain of that.

"Who do you think it could possibly be?" He changed the question just enough to, hopefully, get a different response.

"I already said I don't know." She met his eyes again.

There was frustration and anger in the depth of her gaze and the tilt of her chin. She'd been through a lot. He understood that. He also understood her defensiveness, but if he was going to help her, the walls had to come down, and she needed to be completely open and honest with him.

"My goal isn't to upset you, Kinsley. My goal is to get the truth."

"I've told the truth."

"But have you told all of it?"

They'd reached the station and he waved as Charlotte pulled out of the back lot.

Lights flashing. No siren. She rolled down a window, idling next to the curb as he and Kinsley approached. "Did you see what direction he went?" she asked.

"West on Madison."

"I've put a BOLO out on the vehicle. Hopefully, one of our officers will spot him. I'm heading out." She sped away.

"I hope she finds him," Kinsley sighed. "I'm ready to get back to my normal life."

"I can understand that." He led her around the building and in through a side entrance. He didn't think she'd want to be paraded through the lobby by the chief of police. From what he'd observed, and from what she'd said, he assumed she would prefer not being the center of attention or the subject of speculation.

"Maybe you can," she said quietly. "But I doubt it."

"Why?"

"Because most people don't understand what a privilege it is to live life on your own terms, to make your own decisions about where you go and what you do. They take that freedom for granted. They don't even realize they have it."

"You have a unique perspective, Kinsley. You earned it the hard way, but I do understand not being in control of your schedule and your time. I was in the military for a while. It wasn't prison, but we did follow orders." He stepped into his office, waited for her to enter and then closed the door.

Usually, he'd take victims and witnesses to one of the interview rooms, but he didn't want to bring back bad memories or to make Kinsley feel as if she were being interrogated. He had a few questions to ask, a few things to clarify.

That was all. Maybe once she realized it, she'd relax and be more forthcoming.

"You can have a seat," he said, gesturing to one of two chairs.

She dropped into a chair. "I'm not sure what information you think I'm withholding—"

"I don't recall saying that I thought you were withholding information." He turned on the coffee maker that sat on a file cabinet and took a seat behind the desk.

"Then why am I here?"

"Because you're the victim of a crime, and my office is going to do everything possible to make certain your attacker is apprehended and prosecuted."

Kinsley frowned. "That sounds great, but we both know if you find evidence that you think points in my direction, I'll be as much of a suspect as the guy I picked out of the photo lineup."

"Can I make a suggestion, Kinsley?" he asked.

"Will you withhold it, if I say no?" she responded.

"Probably not."

She smiled, some of the stiffness easing from her posture. "At least you're honest."

"I try to be."

"So, what's your suggestion?"

"Remember you're the victim of a crime.

Don't withhold information because you're worried about being accused of being party to it."

"I'm not withholding information. I'm trying to be reasonable."

"Which means?"

"That the only people who might want to harm me aren't in Montana and, as far as I know, they aren't aware that I'm here."

"As far as you know?"

"I legally changed my name after I was released from prison. There's a lot of notoriety surrounding Kinsley King. Kinsley Garrett is just another person living her life the best way she can. But that's neither here nor there. I changed my name and I left Miami. I didn't tell people where I was going. Most people weren't even aware I was leaving."

"You told no one?" he asked, curious about her life in Miami after she'd been released from prison. She had entered the criminal justice system as a fifteen-year-old kid. She had exited at thirty. The world outside those prison walls had to have been a shock.

"Aside from Elizabeth Harvey, no one knows I'm here."

"Elizabeth is a friend?" Friends talked. He didn't think he needed to point that out.

"I guess you could call her that."

"What would you call her?"

"She was my father's fiancée. She stood by me through the trial. She kept in touch while I was in jail. She let me stay in one of her rental properties when I was released."

"Do you think she'd give your contact information to anyone."

"No." She said it decisively, as if there were no chance that she could be wrong. "But it isn't as if I tried to cover my trail. I'm not difficult to find if someone really wants to do it."

"And who do you think might want to find you?"

"No one really cares enough to, I don't think."

"But if someone did? You are the one who brought up the past, Kinsley. There has to be a reason."

"My uncle. Jay King. He was livid when I was released. He gave a couple of interviews and he made it clear that I belonged in prison, and that he would prefer I rot there."

"Jay King." He jotted the name on his notepad. "He's your father's brother?"

"His twin. I can't imagine him trying to hurt me." She paused, her fingers sliding back and forth across the edge of the desk. She was obviously restless and anxious to be finished.

Marcus was anxious to find the person who seemed determine to kill her. If that meant keeping her in his office for a while longer, if it meant asking tough questions and weeding through difficult-to-decipher answers, that's what he'd do.

"But?" He pressed on, wanting as much information as possible before he called Mr. King.

"He stopped speaking to me after I was arrested. The day I was found guilty, he gave a victim impact statement and told me I deserved to be punished to the full extent of the law. He wanted me sentenced to life without the possibility of parole. He was furious when I was granted a new trial. Furious when I was found innocent." She shrugged. "If you'd asked me twenty years ago if an innocent person could go to prison, I'd have told you no. I would have been wrong. I'm not going to say Uncle Jay would never hurt me even though I don't want to believe he would."

"Do you have his contact information?"

"No, but Elizabeth will. I can give you her number." She rattled it off quickly.

"She won't mind me calling?"

"She'll be happy to help, but…"

"What?"

"I'd rather you not worry her. She's married, has a couple kids, and is a state senator. Her life is hectic. I don't want to add more to it."

"You're asking me not to tell her why I want your uncle's information?"

"I'm telling you that I'd prefer you not give her any more details than necessary."

"That's fine," Marcus said, studying her face, wondering again what it had been like to be released from prison and sent out into unfamiliar world. "Is there anyone else you can think of that might want to harm you?"

"My father's killer."

"Because you're digging into the past? Trying to find out who murdered him?"

"Yes. I hired a private investigative team to look into it," she replied.

His pulse jumped and a shot of adrenaline raced through his blood. She had told him she was keeping files on the investigation, and he had wondered if that might be the reason she was being targeted. "Aside from me, who have you talked to about this?"

"Elizabeth. Doris. If they know, my uncle may. And, of course, anyone the private investigator has interviewed will have heard that I'm looking for the truth."

"Do you know how dangerous what you're doing is? Whoever killed your father probably won't hesitate to kill again."

"My father deserves justice. I want to make certain he gets it. The danger involved doesn't play into it. I started petitioning the Miami police for the case file right after I was released. A year ago, I hired a PI firm to look into his case. They've been calling people who knew my father, getting copies of the file from the police, and probably making things uncomfortable for the murderer."

"This would have been a good thing to mention Saturday night." If she had, he would have already contacted the PI firm, her uncle and Miami police. In law enforcement, it didn't pay to leave stones unturned.

"Saturday night, we both thought I was targeted because of the money I was carrying. It's still possible that is what all this is about. A carjacking that went wrong, and a criminal who doesn't want witnesses to his crime."

"It's possible," he agreed. "But I'd like to speak with the PI firm you hired. If that's okay?"

She gave him a number and a name, her fingers still sliding along the edge of his desk. Her restless energy was making him restless, too.

Marcus reached across and covered her hand with his, stilling the motion.

"Sorry." She pulled her hand back and put it in her lap, her cheeks bright red.

"No need to apologize. I just didn't want you to wear your fingers away." He smiled, hoping to put her at ease. But *ease* wasn't a word he would use to describe her. Kinsley was all coiled muscle and tension, her hands now fisted in her lap, her expression tight and guarded.

"I'm on your side, Kinsley," he said, wondering if she would be able to hear it or if she'd place the words in the same space she put all the information she had received from law enforcement prior to her arrest for her father's murder.

"I know," she murmured, her blush deepening.

"I just need all the facts. Every time. Right away."

"That's what I gave the night my father was murdered. Look what that got me," she replied, standing and stepping away from the desk. "I need to get back to work."

"The bakery is closed for the day," he pointed out. He'd prefer her to stay right where she was until he could escort her to the apartment.

"There's still work that needs to be done. We have to prep for tomorrow."

"I'll walk you back."

"That's not necessary."

"You were nearly run over on your way here. I don't want you walking through town without some security."

"I appreciate your concern, but it isn't going to be possible for a police officer to be with me twenty-four hours a day."

"But it *is* possible for one to be with you now."

She seemed to study his face, maybe looking for some sign that he wasn't sincere or that he had a hidden agenda. He couldn't blame her. She had been railroaded by the criminal justice system at a time when she was the most vulnerable. A healthy amount of caution was to be expected and even applauded.

"In that case, I guess I can't refuse," she finally said.

"You can, but I'm glad you're not going to."

As they stepped into the hall, his radio buzzed, Charlotte's voice cutting through as she called Dispatch to request another patrol car to help with an accident.

He didn't plan to go. There were three officers patrolling the streets.

His cell phone rang. He answered. "Chief Bayne."

"Chief, it's Charlotte. I found the vehicle that almost ran Kinsley down."

"The driver?"

"I believe in the pond. With the vehicle."

"The vehicle is in a pond?"

"Nose down. I can see the tail end but have no visual of the driver."

"What's your location?" He hadn't planned to go, but Charlotte seemed certain the car was the one that had almost run Kinsley down. If that was the case, he wanted to be there if the driver was located.

She gave it quickly.

"I'll be there in ten."

"Everything okay?" Kinsley asked as he tucked the phone into his pocket.

"Change of plans." He switched direction, moving quickly toward the front of the building. Kinsley was nearly running in her effort to keep up. When they reached the front desk, he asked the receptionist, Douglas Morgan, to find an available officer to escort Kinsley to the bakery. As soon as he'd done that, he offered a quick goodbye and ran to his cruiser.

Had the driver escaped?

Was he still in the vehicle?

Had he pushed the car into the pond to keep attention focused away from his escape?

Dozens of questions ran through Marcus's mind as he jumped into the vehicle and sped out of the lot.

SIX

Kinsley had spent the afternoon and evening trying not to think about nearly being run down. Trying not to think about Marcus rushing to the scene of an accident that might have had something to do with her. Trying not to think about anything except ingredients and oven temperature, mixing and baking, checking items off the to-do list that was constantly in her mind.

She'd never been a low-energy person.

Even as a child, she'd enjoyed being busy.

She'd played sports, danced, been involved in theater and art clubs. She'd been a social butterfly, flitting from one group of friends to another. At her trial, those friends had called her spoiled, self-centered, sociopathic. Their opinions had stung almost as much as the accusation of murder.

Prison had caused her to turn that energy inward. She'd attained her GED, gotten a degree in business management and another in art history. She'd taken every class offered by any person who dared breach the walls of the prison to volunteer time with inmates. All those things had helped pass the time and mute her anxiety.

Kinsley had hoped that being released would give her opportunities to pursue old dreams, but those dreams had been the product of a young teen's hopes and ideals. She was older now. Hopefully much wiser. She didn't want the same things she'd wanted then. Wealth didn't interest her. Fancy cars weren't exciting. She still enjoyed being active, but she had no desire to join the church softball team or to engage in group sports activities.

The bakery filled her time and her thoughts.

One day, though, she'd move on.

Once Doris retired, she'd pursue other things.

She had no idea what they would be, but she'd hoped she might find a home in Montana. That maybe she could settle in and create a nice life for herself.

"That can still happen," she mused as she scooped flour from a fifty-pound sack and filled a large plastic container. They'd run out downstairs, and she'd had to climb the steep staircase to refill from the stockroom.

Orders were rolling in.

People were buying product.

Doris was thrilled.

That was what mattered.

Music drifted up from the kitchen. Aside from that, the bakery was silent. Ryker and Madeline had left at seven. Doris had been finally convinced to leave at nine. Kinsley was alone, and that was the way she liked it. She could move at her own pace, get things done in an order that made sense to her. She'd never felt nervous being in the bakery late at night.

The building dated to the late 1800s. It creaked and groaned like any old building, and because it was situated right off Main Street, there were plenty of businesses around. On summer weeknights people were still out at nine and ten o'clock. But it wasn't summer. The sun set early. The weather was still cold. People were tucked away in cozy houses, businesses were closed, and the world outside seemed sinister.

She'd walked to work that morning. Two blocks wasn't far.

But she couldn't imagine walking home.

She closed the bag of flour and lifted the plastic container. She'd finished the last batch of muffins, and she needed to restock ingredients for the morning. After that, she'd could go home.

Only, she wasn't sure she wanted to.

The two blocks there were beginning to seem

like two hundred. An impossible distance to walk alone at ten-thirty at night.

She carried the flour down to the pantry, setting it on the shelf beside the full bin of sugar. That was it. She was finished. Product had been stored in the cooler, ingredients restocked, kitchen and front of the bakery cleaned. Everything was in place for the start of business.

She took off her apron and hung it on a hook near the back door, slid into her coat and grabbed her purse, then ran up front to check the door one last time.

It was closed and locked. Just the way it had been the last three times she'd checked.

She frowned, flicked off the service light and headed back through the store.

Someone knocked and she jumped, her heart racing, her mind numb with fear.

She whirled toward the sound, expecting to see a man with a gun. A masked intruder. Someone bent on harm.

Marcus stood outside, the exterior lights reflecting off his dark hair. He was still in uniform, his coat hanging open to reveal the dark blue slacks and shirt.

Kinsley hurried to open the door, cold air wafting in as he entered.

"What are you doing here?" she asked, realizing how rude that had sounded after she'd already spoken.

"I had an update on your case. I was planning to fill you in tomorrow, but I saw the light go out as I drove past and thought you might be closing up for the night."

"I am."

"I can fill you in now if you have time, or we can wait until tomorrow."

"Now is fine."

"Would you like to do it here? Or I can follow you to the apartment and fill you in there."

"Follow me?"

"You did say you were closing up for the night?"

"I am, but I walked. It might be easier to just walk beside me."

He smiled, the hard angles of his face softening, the fine lines near his eyes deepening. "In that case, how about I give you a ride?"

He was a police officer. *No* seemed like an appropriate answer. The less time she spent around law enforcement, the better she slept at night.

But she had been worried about walking to the apartment alone, and Marcus's offer seemed like the answer to an unspoken prayer. "I'd appreciate that."

"Anything we need to do before you leave?"

"We?" she repeated, and he smiled again.

"I'm here. You can put me to work, if you need to."

"There's nothing left to do."

"Too bad," he murmured as she fished keys out of her purse and led him to the back door.

"Too bad? You want to help in the bakery?"

"I don't want to go home and deal with my niece."

"Is she difficult?"

"I wouldn't say she's difficult. I'd say she's a typical kid who just happens to have a lot of intelligence and a lot of energy. She was in trouble at school again today, and I told my aunt I'd speak with her when I got home."

"What did she do?"

"During art, she created a sign to protest the fact that her teacher won't allow her to read *Lord of the Flies* for her book report."

"How old is she?" Kinsley asked, amused by the thought of a teen or tween protesting a perceived injustice.

"She's seven," he grumbled as they stepped outside.

"Seven? That's young for *Lord of the Flies*."

"I know that. You know that, but my aunt didn't see a problem with it. I think I already told you that my niece's mother—my sister— died eighteen months ago and I'm Rosemarlyn's legal guardian. Her father has never been in the picture."

"That has to be tough on your niece."

"It is, but we're making it work. And my aunt Winnie has stepped in. She moved in after I brought Rosie home. She's a middle-school teacher, and she has a lot more experience with kids than I do."

"I don't have any experience with kids, but her use of art supplies to create a protest sign is a little bit genius," she admitted.

"I thought the same. That's part of the problem."

"How is it a problem to have an intelligent child in school?"

"I asked the same question at the last parent-teacher conference."

"And?"

"I was told that Rosie needs to dial things back and trust the teachers to know what's best for her."

"In other words, she has a lot of energy and her teachers don't like it?"

"Exactly." Marcus chuckled, his fingers brushing her shoulder as he urged her around to the front of the bakery.

His SUV was parked at the curb. He opened the passenger door and waited while she slid in.

A gentleman? Or just someone who went through the motions of being one?

If Kinsley had learned anything from her incarceration, it was that people often weren't what they portrayed themselves to be. Often, they would lie to get what they wanted. They'd betray trust to achieve a goal. And when it came to police officers, they would say just about anything to build trust in someone suspected of a crime.

She hoped that wasn't what Marcus was doing.

He climbed in, started the engine and turned on the heat. "If that's too hot, let me know," he said.

"We're going two blocks," she reminded him.

"Let me know," he repeated, pulling away from the curb.

The bakery looked lonely at night, the lights off, a single bulb above the entrance glowing. If she owned the place, Kinsley would put up more exterior lights. She'd have plants out front and an outside eating area off to the side of the building. She'd have pretty tables and cute umbrellas to keep the sun off customers in the spring and summer and the rain at bay in the fall.

She'd have storefront displays, too. Beautiful faux cakes and pastries to lure people inside.

"I'm sure you're wondering about the update."

Marcus's words broke the silence, bringing back the anxiety she'd been feeling for days. She wanted peace. Probably more than anything else she desired, she craved that. No drama. No chaos. No troubles that couldn't be handled easily.

Suddenly her life had all those things. Drama. Chaos. Major trouble. God's plan was always best. She knew that. Yet she couldn't help but wonder how that plan correlated to her current situation. She'd already been through a lot. Did God really think she needed to go through more?

"I am," she finally responded, terrified of what he would say, worried that somehow, despite all his assurances to the contrary, she was going to become suspect in a crime.

"We found Randy Warren."

"And? Is he talking?"

"He's dead, Kinsley," he said.

"Dead?" she repeated, surprised and sickened by the news.

"He was in the vehicle that went off the road earlier. It matches the make and model of the one that nearly ran you down. The car landed in a pond. His body was found floating near it."

"I'm sorry."

"He tried to kill you and *you're* sorry?"

"I'm sorry he's dead. I'm sorry for the people who love him. Sorry for what they're going to go through the next few days and weeks and months." She knew the heartbreak of loss. She knew the sorrow of saying goodbye to someone. She didn't want that for anyone.

"You've got a good heart," he said, and she felt something she hadn't felt in a long time, something warm and sweet and, maybe, a little exciting.

"I know what it's like to lose someone. Since Randy was driving the car, do you think he's responsible for the fire at my house? Would he really go through all that to keep me from testifying against him?" She pulled the conversation and her focus back to where it needed to be.

"Those are good questions. We're still looking for answers." He turned into the driveway that led to Charlotte's home. The beautiful Victorian was the largest private home on Main Street, the acre of yard setting it apart from its neighbors. Charlotte had given Kinsley a tour the night she'd moved into the apartment above the garage, showing her the upgraded security system and the exterior motion sensor lights. It was as much of a fortress as there could be in a place like Frenchtown, and more secure than Kinsley's house had been.

"So, this isn't over?" she asked.

"Not yet. But it will be." He pulled up in front of the two-story garage, parking next to the stairs that led to the upper level.

"When?"

"As soon as we determine whether or not Randy was acting alone. You did see someone on the road the night you were nearly kidnapped, and we feel confident Randy escaped in a vehicle. We need to find the person who was with him. Once we do that, we should have all the answers we need."

"I understand," she said.

"I wish I had better news."

"It's fine." She twisted the narrow gold band she wore on her right ring finger. It had belonged to her great-grandmother. Since Kinsley's grandmother had never had a daughter, she'd gifted it to Kinsley on her sixteenth birthday, wanting the heirloom to stay in the family. The gift had barely registered. Kinsley had thanked her grandmother but hadn't stopped to appreciate the sentiment behind it. She now wished that she had. There were so many things she wished she had done differently.

"If it's fine, why are you twisting your finger off?" Marcus asked, his finger skimming her knuckle. Her ring finger was red, the area beneath the band raw.

"I'm twisting the ring," she quipped, opening the door and stepping out of the vehicle. She'd felt something when he'd touched her—warmth, curiosity, a desire to find out who Marcus really was, what he was really made of. That scared her. He wasn't just a man. He was a police officer, and she had learned too much about what law enforcement officers would do to prove their versions of the truth.

"It's going to be okay, Kinsley," he said, following her to the staircase that led to her apartment.

"It always is, right?" She headed up the stairs.

"Not always," he responded. "Sometimes we get through but our lives are not the same, and it doesn't feel okay, and it doesn't feel fine."

He was right.

Getting through wasn't the same as being okay.

Accepting something didn't mean it was fine.

She had been irreparably changed by what had happened to her. She didn't like to think about that. She didn't like to face that fact in the mirror every day. She had lost fifteen years of her life. She had lost her father. She had lost her freedom, her trust, her faith in humanity.

All that remained of the girl she'd been was the faith that had been just a mustard seed of belief.

"Want me to come in and check the place out

for you?" Marcus had followed her to the door and was just a few feet away, leaning against the thick metal railing that surrounded the landing.

She should refuse.

She knew that.

Charlotte had security cameras all over her property and alarm systems that were much more advanced than Kinsley's had been. The likelihood that anyone had entered the apartment was slim to none. She could have told him that. She could have sent him on his way. But the night was quiet, the velvety sky sprinkled with stars, the moon hanging just above the horizon, and she didn't want to walk inside alone. Didn't want to be alone.

"I'd appreciate that," she said, unlocking the door.

Marcus wasn't often surprised by people. After so many years of working in law enforcement, he had a sixth sense for subterfuge and a keen eye for the details of people's personalities. If he had been asked to guess whether Kinsley would take him up on his offer, he would have said she wouldn't. From what he had been able to determine, she liked her privacy. She preferred to be alone, and she had spent little to no time fostering friendships in the community. He couldn't blame her for wanting to keep her head down and her connections limited. She had been hurt, and she didn't want to be hurt again. He supposed if he'd been convicted of a crime he hadn't committed, if his friends and some of his family had turned their backs on him, if he'd finally been freed and learned that the community still viewed him as suspect, he'd be defensive and solitary, too.

So, yeah. He was surprised that she'd accepted his offer. He didn't tell her that as she punched a code into the security box on the inside wall and flipped on a light.

He followed her into a large open-concept room.

A kitchen area took up part of it, the appliances stainless steel, the floor scuffed hardwood. A small nook, built out from the kitchen, contained bookshelves and a desk and chair centered on a small area rug. The living area took up the rest of the space with a sectional sofa, an easy chair and a television.

"Nice place," he said as she kicked off her shoes and walked into the living area.

"It was nice of Charlotte to let me stay here."

"Nice? Charlotte? The people she arrests wouldn't call her that," he joked.

"Would the people you arrest call you nice?"

"I hope not."

She smiled, but he could feel her nervous en-

ergy as she paced across the room and opened a
door that led into a narrow hall. "The bathroom,
laundry room and storage closet are in here.
There's no entry except the front door and the
windows. Charlotte does have a fire escape on
the window at the end of the hall, but it's inter-
nal. A ladder that I can lower if there's an emergency." She was speaking quickly, the words
tumbling over themselves as she walked into
the hall.

"You don't need to be nervous around me,"
Marcus said as she opened a door and stepped
into a bathroom. Tan walls. White and chrome.
Not fancy but comfortable and new.

"Don't I?" she murmured, sidling past him
and stepping back into the hall.

"Why would you?"

"Because you're a police officer and I'm always nervous around the police?"

"Right now, I'm off duty. The only thing I
am is a friend."

"We barely know each other, so friendship is
difficult to believe."

"Neighbor? Does that suit you better?" He
walked into the laundry room with its single
window that looked too small for a grown person to climb in through or out of. Another small
room contained a vacuum, cleaning supplies
and a few closed and taped boxes.

"We still barely know each other," she pointed out. "You're nearly a stranger, and you're in my apartment. That was something you warned us about in self-defense class. So, of course, I'm nervous. According to your class, I should be."

He checked the back window. It was locked, fire escape ladder sitting on a small trunk beneath it. "I do warn about things like this in the class, but I think you know enough about me to know I'd never hurt you."

He turned.

Kinsley was a few feet away, her black slacks and purple button-up shirt dusted with flour from a day at the bakery. Some of her hair had escaped, long tendrils falling against her neck, the strands bright red against her pale skin.

She was a beautiful woman. He'd noticed that the first time he'd seen her. He'd also noticed how young she'd looked. He'd assumed she was a college student taking a self-defense class to help her stay safe on campus. Later, he'd noticed the fine lines at the corners of her eyes and the maturity she possessed.

"You're staring." She frowned, her eyes nearly hidden by bangs that had escaped clips and were falling onto her face.

"Just trying to figure out what I can do to make you more comfortable."

"Leave?"

He didn't laugh because he didn't think she was joking. "I have a better idea."

"What?"

"Come to my place tomorrow for dinner. You can meet my aunt and niece and get to know my family."

She frowned. "Come to your house for dinner?"

"That *is* what I said," he replied.

"How is that going to make me more comfortable?"

"I figure once we get to know each other, we won't be strangers any longer, and you won't need to be so guarded around me."

"Does dinner include an interrogation?" she queried, a frown line between her brows.

"Why would it?'

"Because you're a police officer. That doesn't just get turned off when you go home at night."

It was true, and he wouldn't deny it. Before Rosmarlyn had become part of his life, he hadn't ever turned the police officer off. Now, he tried to separate his private life from his job. *Tried.*

He wasn't always successful.

Lately, he'd been less successful than usual. Kinsley's case had been weighing on his mind, keeping him up at night as he'd tried to put the pieces together to create a cohesive picture of what was going on.

"No interrogation. You're not a suspect. You're a victim. You have nothing to worry about."

She studied his face, her eyes vivid blue. The freckles on her nose and cheeks added to the illusion of youth, but that she was closing in on thirty-five, that she had lived a difficult life, that she had earned the faint lines on her forehead and at the corners of her eyes.

"I probably shouldn't do this..." she intoned. "But dinner with your family sounds nice."

"Why should you 'probably not'?" Marcus asked, surprised at how happy her answer made him. He hadn't had a woman over for more than two years. He'd issued the invitation because he'd thought she needed more connection in the community. She seemed to be drifting, and he wanted her to feel like she was part of something.

"If you haven't noticed, I've made a habit of keeping to myself," she replied.

"Because?"

"Isn't it obvious? My life is like a docudrama of betrayal and disappointment."

"And triumph," he pointed out.

"That, too, though it won't be total triumph

until I find the person who killed my father and until I know that justice is finally being served."

"It's a shame it wasn't served properly eighteen years ago."

"I want to say that the police did the best they could."

"But you don't believe it."

"I was the easy suspect. The spoiled teen daughter who stood to gain a lot of money if her father died. But the footprints they found in the backyard were of a size ten men's shoe. They found male DNA on one of the glasses sitting on the coffee table. My father had obviously let the killer in. It was someone he knew. But the killer wasn't me."

"They didn't have much evidence against you. I've read the case file."

"They had enough to convict me. My fingerprints were on the gun. My DNA was all over him. I had his blood on my clothes. I'd tried to do CPR. I thought I could save him." Her voice broke.

"I'm sorry."

"You've said that before. It's not your fault."

"A failure of the justice system feels like the fault of everyone who works in it." He walked to the door. "You have my number if you need anything, right?"

"Yes," she replied. "But Charlotte lives a

hundred yards away. She can probably get here more quickly if there's trouble."

"She's working tonight. I have officers running patrol past the house, but keep my number handy. Just in case." He stepped out onto the landing. "I don't want you to live in fear, Kinsley. You've gone through enough. It's time for peace."

"Funny you say that. When I left prison, I told Doris there were only two things I wanted. Justice and peace. I knew it would be difficult to get justice, but I didn't think peace would be so hard to come by." She smiled, but he could see the pain in her eyes and the disillusionment in her face.

Marcus tried to keep his distance when he worked a case. It didn't pay to get emotionally involved, but Kinsley's situation made him want to make amends. She made him want to get involved in a way he hadn't been before.

They were neighbors.

That was the excuse he gave himself for stepping closer, for letting his hands settle on her shoulders and his palms smooth across tense muscles. "I'm going to do everything I can to make sure you have both those things."

"I appreciate that, Marcus, but those are things I'm going to have to find myself."

"It isn't a bad thing to let people help. As a

matter of fact, sometimes that's the only way to make it through. How does six sound for dinner? I'll pick you up. Until we find Randy's accomplice, it's better if you don't spend a lot of time outside alone."

"All right. I appreciate it. Good night."

She turned, walked inside the house and closed the door.

He waited until he heard the soft swish of the bolt sliding home and then jogged down the stairs and climbed into his SUV.

Marcus understood what Kinsley was saying. It was true that she would have to seek those things herself, but that didn't mean she couldn't have a little help along the way.

SEVEN

What did a person wear to have dinner with neighbors?

Kinsley should have known the answer.

By this time in her life, she should have had plenty of experience socializing with a variety of people. She should have a logbook of information in her head—all the societal rules and niceties. Instead, she was clueless, staring at the few items of clothing she'd bought after the fire and trying to decide which was more appropriate for the occasion.

Her phone rang as she unfolded a peacock-blue sweater.

She answered quickly, her mind still spinning through her options, her thoughts on her impending dinner with Marcus and his family. All the other things—the death of Randy, the police search for his accomplice, her concern that everything that was happening might be tied to her past—pushed to the side for the evening.

"Hello?"

"Kinsley?" a man asked.

"Yes. Who am I speaking with?"

"Jay. Your uncle."

"Jay?" Shocked, she dropped onto the sofa, her knees wobbly, legs shaky. The last time she had spoken to him had been before her sentencing. He'd been allowed to read a victim's impact statement. She had begged him to believe in her innocence.

"I'm sure you're surprised." The words were clipped, his tone terse.

"I am. I didn't realize you had my number." A million words wanted to bubble out, dozens of questions demanded to be voiced, but she shoved them down.

"Elizabeth said you were having some trouble. She thought this might be a good time for me to reach out to you."

"What trouble?" she asked. She hadn't told Elizabeth about the near kidnapping. She certainly hadn't told her about the murder attempts. It was possible Doris had. Kinsley had asked her not to, but Doris believed a woman of her age should be able to say and do what she wanted.

"A carjacking. Stolen money? Your house set on fire?"

"I've had a few problems. Nothing that I can't handle"

"So, it's true?"

"It's nothing for you or Elizabeth to worry about. I've tried to keep as much of it from her as possible. Doris must be passing along information." She'd have to talk to Doris about that. She had purposely kept information from Elizabeth. She hadn't wanted her to worry.

"It sounds worrisome to me."

"Things are fine. The police have everything under control."

"You're sure? No matter what has happened, you're still my niece. If you need help, I'll give it. For Michael's sake."

"I'm sure."

"All right. Good. Glad to hear things are okay." Kinsley could hear the relief in his voice and realized he must be worried that he had an obligation as her father's brother to step in if she were in real trouble.

She couldn't lie, but she didn't need more drama. And she didn't want him entering her life, carrying his anger and resentment with him. She might long to reconnect, but if reconnecting meant dealing with the vitriol he'd flung at her during her sentencing hearing, she'd pass.

"I wish Elizabeth hadn't given you my number."

"You're my niece."

"That's not what you said at the sentencing

hearing." Kinsley could hear the hurt in her voice and feel it in the pit of her stomach. She'd thought she was past it, but maybe it had just been lying dormant.

"My brother is dead. That can't be changed. But the older I get, the more I realize I don't want to lose my niece, as well," he responded. Same clipped, terse tenor. If he had softened toward her, she couldn't tell by his tone.

"You didn't lose me. You shoved me out of your life," she pointed out, her throat raw with tears she was trying to hold back. She had loved Uncle Jay. He'd been a fun version of her father. Always energetic. Always enthusiastic. He'd attended all her sports events. He'd been to her piano recitals. He'd taken her to the gun range for the first time. Taught her gun safety and how to load and fire a pistol.

He'd been a key witness for the prosecution at her father's trial, testifying to her familiarity with a firearm and her accuracy with gun.

"I'm flying into Montana on Saturday evening. I booked a hotel in Missoula. I'd like to see you, if that's possible."

"Why?" she asked, the thick, hot feeling in her throat growing, her eyes burning. Jay had been family. Then he had turned his back on her.

"I already told you why. My brother is gone.

My parents are gone. I have no children. You're the only family I have left. I'll call you when I arrive. No need to pick me up at the airport. I rented a car." He disconnected.

For a moment, Kinsley didn't move. Her heart thudded in her ears, her body seeming to hum with useless energy.

She'd dreamed about reconnecting with Uncle Jay.

She'd spent hours penning letters that begged him to believe in her innocence. She'd mailed them and never received a reply. He had cut her off completely. If she hadn't been released from prison, she didn't think she'd have ever heard from him again.

She wasn't sure how she felt about meeting with him.

He and her father were identical twins.

Seeing him would be like seeing her dad.

Alive. Aged. Changed by all the years apart.

But there.

Kinsley would give everything she had for that to happen. She would go back to prison if that meant her father lived and she could see him again.

Tears slipped down her cheeks.

She brushed them away impatiently. She had spent her first few years in prison crying herself to sleep. It hadn't done any good. It certainly hadn't changed her circumstances. Eventually, she had realized she needed to forget the past and work toward the future.

Kinsley changed quickly, tears still falling. All the memories she had shoved into the farthest recesses of her mind suddenly right there. Waiting for her to acknowledge them.

She'd had a happy life, a blessed one.

And then everything had changed.

She wanted to know why.

Her father had been well liked. He'd been an FBI agent. He'd had people who might want to harm him, but the police had ruled the possibility of a retaliatory attack slim. He'd been shot by someone he'd allowed into the house. Killed by someone he'd trusted. No matter how many ways she looked at it, Kinsley couldn't think of anyone in his life who would have wanted to harm him.

Someone knocked on the door, the gentle rap startling her from her thoughts. She walked to the door and peered out the peephole. Marcus stood on the landing, his dark hair nearly covered by a cowboy hat, his hand shoved into the pocket of his coat.

He smiled when she opened the door. She'd expected him to be in uniform, but he was wearing a pair of faded jeans, a dark blue plaid shirt and work boots. His hair was a little long, the ends curling near the collar of his coat. When he met her eyes, her heart jumped. Just the way it had when she'd seen her high school crush for the first time.

Only, she wasn't in high school.

She wasn't going to allow herself to have a crush.

"Hi," she breathed, turning away, afraid of what she'd see in his eyes. "I'm almost ready. Sorry, I'm running a little behind. I just need to grab my coat and purse, and we can go."

"What's wrong?" he asked, stepping into the apartment and closing the door. The quiet click should have panicked her. She hated when other people closed doors on her. She hated feeling penned in and locked up.

"Nothing," she lied, grabbing her purse without meeting his eyes. She didn't want to see compassion in his face. She didn't want to accept empathy. She had learned to be strong in prison. She wouldn't allow herself to be weak.

"Then why are you crying?"

"I'm not." That was the truth. Her eyes were dry but burning, her throat tight with unshed tears.

He touched her arm, his fingers curling lightly around her biceps. No pressure. Just urging her to turn and face him.

"What's wrong, Kinsley?"

"My uncle called."

"The one who doesn't speak to you because he believes you killed your father?"

"I only have one uncle…so, yes."

"I didn't think he had your contact information."

"He didn't. Elizabeth gave it to him."

"Against your wishes?"

"I didn't ever expressly ask her not to, but I'm surprised that she did."

"What did your uncle want?" Marcus asked, a frown lining his brow, his eyes filled with concern.

"He said he's flying into Missoula on Saturday. He rented a hotel room, and he wants to see me while he's there."

"That's a surprise."

"I thought so."

"Do you plan to see him?"

"I haven't decided yet."

"Can I make a suggestion?"

"Can I stop you?" she asked.

"Probably not." Marcus smiled.

Her heart skipped a beat. Her stomach summersaulted.

For a moment, Kinsley's mind went blank. All she could do was stare into his eyes. He was a gorgeous man with a good heart. A person of strong convictions and values. She shouldn't be surprised that she was attracted to him.

But she was.

Plenty of men came into the bakery. She saw men every Sunday at church. Single and available men who weren't law enforcement officers. Guys who had asked her out or tried to get to know her better. She had turned them all away.

She had thought she was past the years of longing for companionship. She'd been wrong.

"Go ahead, then. What's your advice?"

"Don't meet with him alone." His smile had faded, his expression turning serious.

"I can't take Doris with me, and Elizabeth is in Florida. If I don't meet with him alone, I won't be meeting with him at all."

"You forgot about me," he said, opening the closet and pulling out her coat.

"You?"

"I could go with you to meet him. As a matter of fact, I'd like to."

"I couldn't ask you to do that."

"You didn't ask. I offered." He held out her coat and helped her into it, his knuckles brushing her neck as he adjusted the collar.

Warmth spread from her neck to her cheeks, her body suddenly humming with awareness. He was a man. She was a woman. They were standing so close, she could see the fine lines near his eyes and a tiny scar on his chin. If she wanted to, she could step back. But she stayed. Looking into his eyes, reading compassion and understanding in his face.

Life had been short on those things for a long time.

To see them, to feel them in the warmth of his hands as they rested on her shoulders, to know that he was willing to do what it took to keep her safe, mattered more than Kinsley wanted to admit.

She wasn't in Montana to find companionship.

But what if she did?

What if she walked into it the same way she'd walked into trouble years ago? What if God had put her on a path that would lead to something she hadn't anticipated? Or even wanted?

"It's okay to let me help you," Marcus said quietly.

"Why would you want to? Because I was the victim of a crime in your town? Because I was railroaded by the justice system eighteen years ago? You don't owe me anything, Marcus, and I don't want you to feel beholden to me because of things you had nothing to do with."

"I don't feel anything except concern. If something were to happen to you on a Saturday night, no one would know about it until you didn't show up for work Monday morning."

He was right. She couldn't argue his point. She didn't check in with Doris every day. She attended church, but they went to different services. "All right. If I meet with him, you can come."

"Thank you," he said, opening the door so she could step into the crisp evening air. Her shoulder brushed his arm as she moved, and she was reminded of long-ago times and childhood crushes; of the easy days where it felt natural and right to spend time alone with a man.

Kinsley hadn't thought she would ever want to revisit that.

She'd been certain that she would spend the rest of her life living alone and going it alone. Being close to people hurt. Counting on people opened a person up to betrayal. She didn't think she had the strength to face disappointments again.

"Are you okay?" he asked as she led the way down the stairs.

"I'm fine."

"You're sure? If you'd rather not come to dinner, I understand. Rosie can be a handful, and her energy level can be a little off-putting."

"To whom?" she asked, glad they'd changed the direction of the conversation.

"Her teachers mostly."

"Maybe she needs more tolerant teachers?"

"According to them, she needs a little less energy and enthusiasm."

"I can't see anything wrong with either of those things."

"Me neither. But in the classroom, I understand they have to be reined in."

"I'm not a teacher. Your home isn't a classroom. I'm sure I can handle Rosie."

"That makes one of us," he muttered.

"She's giving you a run for your money, huh?"

"That's one way to put it."

"What's another way?"

"She's giving me gray hair and sleepless nights. The way I see things, if Rosie's like this at seven, I might not survive her teen years."

"Is she really that bad?"

"She isn't at all bad. She's just busy. She's likely to talk your ear off, and if you're already tired, that may be too much."

"Who says I'm tired?"

"The dark circles under your eyes," he said, opening the door of the SUV and holding it while Kinsley got in.

"Thanks for pointing them out," she said, more amused by his comment than anything else.

"Any time," he said, winking as he closed the door.

She watched him walk around the SUV, waited while he climbed in, told herself that he wasn't any different than any other man she'd met.

Her heart was saying something different.

It was saying that he wasn't like anyone else she'd ever met.

That, if she wasn't careful, she might just fall for him.

Marcus expected dinner to be chaotic. Rosie loved attention, and she loved talking. Highly intelligent and extremely active, she tended to wear out her welcome whenever they visited other homes. When people came to their home, she had to be reminded over and over again to keep her voice down and to wait her turn to talk.

This time, he noted with amusement, she had been awed into silence by Kinsley's red hair. Apparently, it reminded her of a Disney princess whose name he couldn't remember.

After dinner, Kinsley helped to clear the table. Then she'd dried the dishes that Winnie washed while Marcus and Rosie had put away the leftovers. The rhythm of movement, the way they interacted, reminded him of his childhood and the evening meals he'd had with his parents and sister. They'd been a team, working together for a common goal.

After their deaths, Winnie had done the best she could. She had tried to recreate the family structure, and she had been largely successful. But she'd also been working two jobs, struggling to pay bills and to keep food on the table. There had been no life insurance. No savings accounts. Nothing to draw on except her determination to keep Marcus and Jordyn together.

He hadn't realized that until he was an adult.

Winnie had never complained and never acted as if caring for them was a burden. It wasn't until he'd become an adult that he'd thought about what she had given up to make that happen. She'd had her entire life stretched out ahead of her, dozens of possibilities, plenty of interested men. Overnight, everything had changed.

"You made a delicious meal, Marcus. Just like always. I'd love to stay for a while longer, but I have plans," Winnie said as she dried her hands on a towel.

"Plans?" He knew he sounded surprised. He *was* surprised. In the year and a half since she had moved in to help him with Rosie, she hadn't gone anywhere except work and church meetings.

"Yes. Plans. I'll be back in an hour. I'm sorry to eat and run, Kinsley."

"There's no need to apologize. It was a pleasure meeting you, Winnie."

"I feel the same. I'll see you when I get back. I know Marcus is giving you a ride home, so I won't be longer than an hour."

"Can't I come, Aunt Winnie?!" Rosie asked, jumping up and down as if afraid she wouldn't be heard if she didn't.

"Not this time, sugarplum," Winnie replied.

"I am not a sugarplum. I'm a superhero," Rosie announced as she threw her arms around Winnie.

Kinsley laughed.

She was more relaxed than he'd ever seen her, her expression soft and unguarded. He could imagine her as she'd been before she'd gone to prison. Young. Happy. Excited by life and everything the future had to offer.

Winnie walked to the door and opened it, her gaze cutting to Marcus before she left. She was sending an unspoken message. He was certain he knew exactly what she was saying. *Don't mess this up.*

As if he was starting something.

As if the invitation to dinner was something other than him wanting to get to know the neighbor.

Maybe it was. Maybe Winnie knew the things he didn't want to admit to himself—that he was getting older and that the bachelor life didn't have as much appeal as it had when he was fresh out of the military. After his fiancée had been killed, he had been sure he would never fall in love again. Never marry. Never have a family of his own. He had been determined to live his life single. No commitment. No chance of having his heart shattered again.

But lately he wondered if that was the right choice.

If maybe the risk of losing someone would be worth it for the rewards love brought.

"You know what I think?" Rosie asked.

"What?" Kinsley responded before he could.

"We should go outside and look for buried treasure. I was reading *Treasure Island*, and it seems to me there are treasures everywhere."

"Treasure hunting?" Kinsley glanced at Marcus, her eyes such a deep blue he almost forgot what they were discussing.

"That sounds like fun, but you have homework, Rosie."

"I do not have homework. I finished everything at school," she declared, her curly hair bouncing with the force of her indignation.

"If I call Mrs. Price, will she tell me the same thing?"

Rosie scowled, her eyes flashing with ire.

"But, Uncle Marcus, you can't call my teacher. She's at home."

"She gave me her home number," he countered, wishing it wasn't true.

"But she's probably sleeping."

"Rosmarlyn, are you fibbing about homework again?" he asked.

As was her way, she crumbled, her dark eyes filling with tears, her bottom lip poking out. She was a high-energy child with a very soft heart. "I have some reading and some math."

"Sit down and get it done, then. Once you're finished, we can treasure hunt."

"But Kinsley might not be here. It'll only be fun, if she is."

"I can stick around long enough to hunt for treasures," Kinsley said. "As long as your uncle doesn't mind."

"Really? Awesome!" Kinsley darted into the den. Marcus could hear her book bag opening and papers being shuffled around.

"She's a sweet kid," Kinsley said, the soft expression still on her face.

"She is. I hope I don't ruin her."

"Why would you?"

"Because I know nothing about children and zero about girls."

"You had a sister and an aunt. You know

something about girls," she corrected with a smile.

"That still leaves me with the fact that I know nothing about children," he replied, studying the way her face looked when she smiled.

Kinsley must have noticed his scrutiny. She turned away, hiding her expression as she made a show of looking at the photos hung on the wall. Most were pictures of Jordyn and Rosie, taken from their apartment.

"Jordyn was lovely," she said. "Rosie favors her."

"And my mother." Marcus touched a picture of the family the year his parents had been killed.

"That's you when you were a boy?" She turned to face him again, and he realized how close they were. Barely a foot between them. She had to crane her neck to meet his eyes, her bangs falling nearly to her cheekbones.

"It is."

"You were a cute kid."

"I was a handful," he replied, wondering how they had come to this place where they were both standing in his family room, barely a foot between them. He could reach out and brush her bangs from her face, let his fingers trail down her temple and along the curve of her cheekbone.

He clenched his fists to stop himself.

"Like Rosie?" she asked.

"I hadn't thought about it, but I guess so. I remember my parents going to the school several times when I was young. I was busy, and I didn't like sitting at a desk."

"There's a lot of desk work when you're a police officer."

"I grew into tolerating it. I still prefer to be on patrol, but reports have to be written."

"My father used to say two-thirds of his job was paperwork."

"I'd say that's accurate. You and your father were close, weren't you?" he asked.

"Very. It was just me and my father and my grandparents for most of my life." She sat on the love seat.

He almost took the seat next to her. There was plenty of room, but he didn't want to make her nervous or to send her running. He chose the recliner instead.

"And your uncle."

"Yes. My uncle." Kinsley frowned. "I had so much fun with your family, I almost forgot about his visit."

"And now that you've remembered, you're nervous again?"

"Nervous? Terrified."

"Of?"

"That we'll revisit all the stuff he said during my sentencing hearing, and that the things that I'm too afraid to hope for won't happen."

"Reconciliation?"

"Yes."

"Have you ever wondered if he could be responsible for your father's death?"

Her silence stretched out for so long, Marcus worried he'd offended her.

Finally, she sighed. "I want to say no."

"But?"

"But it's been there. In the back of my mind."

"That he might have been involved."

"Yes. He had an airtight alibi, yet he also had a lot to gain if I was out of the picture."

"Which is what ended up happening."

"Yes. Uncle Jay was executor of my father's will. I was the sole beneficiary of his life insurance policy. If something happened to me, Jay would receive the funds."

"Something did happen to you. You went to jail."

"Right. For my dad's murder. That meant there was no payout from the private insurance he'd purchased, but he also had a life insurance policy through the FBI. Uncle Jay was co-beneficiary. My father left him half that money."

"And if something happened to you, he got it all?"

"Yes, but he put my half in an account and never touched it. Not any of it. I always thought it was because my grandparents were watching him, making sure he didn't take what my father meant for me. Once they passed away, there was nothing stopping him from using it. But, when I was released from prison, he sent me a check." She twisted a strand of hair around her finger.

"So, he wasn't after the money?"

"I don't think so. After my grandparents died, he didn't try to go after my inheritance."

"Another life insurance policy?"

"My father's parents each had one. They were also well-off financially. Despite everything they spent trying to free me." She stood and paced to the window that looked out into the front yard.

"This isn't something I enjoy talking about. The presumption of the prosecution in my case was that I killed my father for money, and because I was tired of living by his rules. They had enough physical evidence to make a case, so they stuck with that theory and prosecuted me."

"Fingerprints on a gun and DNA aren't all that much evidence. You lived in the same house."

"And I had been to the shooting range with my father a few days prior. They didn't find gun powder residue on my hands, but they thought the blood splatter on my shirt happened when I fired the weapon at close range, and I could have been wearing gloves when I fired the shots. My defense attorney argued that the blood splatter occurred while I did CPR, but the jury didn't buy that."

"They should have."

"Would you?" she asked. "If you were sitting in the jury box, would you have believed that I just happened to be out at a party the night my father was killed? That I just happened to have touched the gun that was used a few days prior? That I just happened to get blood splatter from doing CPR? There was no evidence that a stranger had been in the house. The only DNA evidence collected from my father's body was mine."

"I don't know what I would have believed," he admitted.

"I don't know what I would have believed either. I sat in the courtroom and listened to the case against me, and if I hadn't known I was innocent, even I might have believed the lies. The fact is, I understand why the prosecutors went after me. My father had a large life insurance policy, and I was a spoiled, bratty kid. But money isn't a kiss good-night before bed. It isn't an I-love-you as you run out the door. It isn't a text that says 'I miss you.' Money makes it easy to buy things, but things can't replace people. They can't replace family and friends and warm embraces."

"I can't imagine going through what you did," Marcus said. He crossed the room, touched her arm. That was all he meant to do. Just a quick assurance that he was there.

But she met his eyes. He could see the hurt and betrayal there, the young girl who had been naive enough to believe the system always worked and that it always protected the innocent.

He pulled her close, wrapping his arms around her. Her head rested against his chest, her hair a silky rope sliding over his hands as he stroked her back and told her again how sorry he was.

"Does this mean you're getting married?" Rosie said so loudly that Kinsley jumped.

"No!" she replied, obviously appalled by the idea.

He should have been, too.

He was a diehard bachelor, a guy who enjoyed his freedom, but he was beginning to realize that freedom wasn't all it was cracked up to be.

"It means we're friends," he said, his gaze still on Kinsley.

"Too bad," Rosie said with an exaggerated sigh. "I need a woman in my life."

"You have Winnie," Kinsley said.

"She's my aunt. And not even my aunt. She's my *great*-aunt. Which means she's old."

"She's only ten years older than me," Marcus pointed out.

"I saw some gray in your hair last night when you were reading me a book. Maybe you're old, too."

"Rosemarlyn, that's enough of the 'old' talk," he muttered.

"I'm just saying that I need a young woman in my life. Like, Mommy's age. Someone who can tell me all the stuff I need to know about growing up. A kid shouldn't have to figure that stuff out on her own."

"You're not going to have to figure anything out on your own," he assured her, surprised that she'd mentioned her mother. In the year and a half since she'd moved in, she hadn't once talked about Jordyn.

His cell phone rang and he took it out of his pocket to glance at the number.

Charlotte. Unusual on a night that he wasn't working. "I need to get this," he said. "I'll just be a minute."

He stepped into the den and answered. "Bayne here. What's up?"

"We just had a call from one of my neighbors. Suspicious activity at my place. They thought they saw someone wandering around near the house. I'm heading there now, but thought you'd want to know since Kinsley is in the apartment."

"She's currently at my place."

"Is she? At least we know she's safe. I'll check things out and get back to you." Charlotte disconnected, but he wasn't content to sit and wait. If the person they were looking for was found at Kinsley's apartment, he wanted to be there for the interview.

He glanced at his watch, trying to gauge how long it would be before Winnie returned.

"Do you need to go?" Kinsley asked.

"When Winnie gets home."

"If you need to leave now, I can stay with Rosie," she offered.

He didn't plan to take her up on it. She was there for dinner. Not to babysit.

"I really don't mind. To be honest, this is the first time in a long time that I've felt almost... normal."

He would have asked her what she meant, but Winnie hurried through the front door.

"I heard there was trouble at Charlotte's house. I thought I'd better come back. Just in case you needed to go," she announced.

"How did you hear?" he asked, still not planning to leave.

Work was important.

The case was important.

But, he didn't want to abandon Kinsley to his family.

"From a friend. You'd better get out of here. Kinsley and I can spend more time getting to know each other while you sort things out."

"I have officers who can handle it," he responded.

"You want to be there, so go. I'll be fine with your family until you get back." Kinsley smiled. Strands of hair had escaped the ponytail she'd pulled them into. They clung to her neck and sild over her shoulders. Looking into her eyes, he had a glimpse of a future he hadn't ever wanted, hadn't dreamed of, had never imagined could exist—a woman saying goodbye to him in the morning, waiting for him to return home at night, encouraging him to pursue his job with all of his heart and passion.

And, his heart telling him to always make room for her.

Surprised, he stepped back, grabbed his coat, said a rushed goodbye and hurried outside. The cold air cooled his skin, but did nothing to clear his head. He was still imagining those things, still thinking about how easy it would be to include someone like Kinsley in his life as he hopped into his SUV and headed for Charlotte's place.

EIGHT

Having a seven-year-old around was a great distraction, but despite endless games of Go Fish and a treasure hunt adventure in the yard, Kinsley's mind kept returning to the phone call Marcus had received.

If someone had been trying to get into the apartment, he would have had a difficult time. Charlotte had top-notch locks and security systems. The apartment was cozy, and Kinsley was happy there. The company she'd hired to clean and restore her house had given a four-week estimate for the length of the job. Elizabeth had suggested she move into a bigger place while she waited. She'd said a month was a long time to be in such a small place.

It was nothing in comparison to being in a prison cell for fifteen years. As long as she had her freedom, Kinsley would be happy almost anywhere.

"All right. That's it. Time for bed, Rosie," Winnie said as she scooped up the playing cards.

"But it's early," Rosie argued, her dark eyes flashing with energy. Marcus had been right. She rarely stopped moving and talking, but when she was focused, her focus couldn't be broken.

"It's late," Winnie corrected.

"Uncle Marcus—"

"Don't even try it," Winnie warned. "Go hop into bed. I'll tuck you in shortly."

To her credit, Rosie didn't argue further. She stopped next to Kinsley, gave her a quick hug and a kiss on the cheek and bounced up the stairs.

"She's very sweet," Kinsley said.

"She is. Marcus thinks she's like his sister, but she's more like him. Always into mischief but with the best heart. Jordyn never got into trouble when she was young. Then she became an older teen and decided to experiment." Winne stood. Tall and curvy with raven-black hair and gray-blue eyes, she didn't look a decade older than Marcus.

"That must have been hard."

"It was. It still is. I feel like I could have done things differently and, if I had, Jordyn would still be around." She sighed. "I'd better go tuck Rosie in. If I don't, she'll be up staring out the window and imagining traveling to space until I do." She jogged up the stairs.

Kinsley listened to the soft hum of voices drifting from somewhere above. She'd spent years longing for silence. The constant noise of prison life had made relaxing difficult and sleep nearly impossible. Now, she enjoyed the quiet of living alone. In the evening, she listened to the white noise of the freezer and the hushed whoosh of the heating system. She played music or turned on the television to fill the emptiness with sound.

This was nice.

Sitting at a kitchen table while life was carried out in other parts of the house. It reminded her of her childhood, her grandparents watching television while she worked on her homework and they all waited for her father to come home.

She missed those days.

A murderer had stolen the years she should have spent with her father. The criminal justice system had taken the last years she could have had with her grandparents.

And now life seemed empty, her only focus on justice she wasn't certain she would ever get. She'd been out of prison for nearly three years. She had grown nothing except a pile of files and information about her father's murder. She didn't have friends. Her only family despised her. Doris and Elizabeth were still part of her life, but they had homes and people they loved. She would only ever be on the periphery of that.

Her cell phone rang, and she pulled it out of her handbag. Elizabeth's number was on the screen. She answered, surprised to hear from her so late on a weekend night. "Hello?"

"Kins? It's Elizabeth. How are you, dear?"

"I'm good. Is everything okay?"

"Right as rain. I called the bakery, thinking you'd be there late tonight. No one picked up."

"Saturday isn't a late night. We're closed on Sunday, remember?" She was surprised that Elizabeth had made the mistake. She'd always been rigid about schedules and time. She kept detailed calendars and referred to them frequently.

"Ah. That's right. It's been a hectic week. Forgive my old brain. You're still in the apartment? I haven't missed an announcement about you returning home, have I?"

"No. I'm still at the apartment. Although, I'm having dinner with friends tonight."

"Friends plural, so that means it's not a date. Too bad. I won't keep you, dear, but I need to let you know what I've done. I hope you're not too upset with me." She had a deep voice with just a hint of a rasp in it. In the courtroom, she had a commanding presence that had earned her the reputation of being a bulldog for the prosecution. Now that she'd become a state senator, she'd toned down the hard edges and softened her approach.

Or maybe time had done that for her.

"Is this about the fact that you gave my number to Uncle Jay?" Kinsey hinted, swinging around as the front door opened. Cold air blasted through the room as Marcus stepped inside. He smiled, and her pulse jumped.

"Has he reached out to you already?" Elizabeth asked.

Kinsley was so distracted by Marcus, it took a moment for the question to register. When it did, she hurried to answer. "Yes. Tonight. He says he's flying out here."

"Did he give you the song and dance about wanting to reconnect?"

"Song and dance?" Kinsley said. Marcus had stepped closer. There were flecks of snow melting in his hair. She had the urge to smooth it down and to rub some warmth into his hands.

"That's what he told me. That he wanted to reconnect with you. You're his only family, and he doesn't want your relationship to be broken over something you did when you were fifteen."

"I didn't do anything when I was fifteen except go to a party without permission," she nearly barked, all the years of defending herself and trying to convince people that she was innocent welling up and spilling out in her tight, hard words.

"I know that. You know that. But Jay doesn't. He thinks he's being magnanimous by reaching out to you. I guess he's decided that God wants him to forgive. Wasn't sure I believed him but—"

"If you didn't believe his story, why did you give him my number and tell him where I was?" Kinsey asked, turning away because she didn't want to see the sympathy and curiosity in Marcus's eyes.

"Because I'm ever the optimist. It's possible he's being sincere, and I'm just being a cynic. After years of prosecuting guilty people who looked people straight in the face while insisting they were innocent, I tend to expect people to lie."

"I didn't lie."

"You're an exception to the rule, honey. Because your father raised you to be honest. It's a great quality. Most of the time. Anyway, Jay may have been difficult in the past, but he is your father's twin. Michael would be heartbroken if he knew that the two of you were estranged."

That was true.

She knew it, but she still wasn't happy that Jay had been given her contact information.

"I just wish you would have asked first, Elizabeth."

"Next time, I will. I just…get nostalgic sometimes. I miss what we had all those years ago." There was something in her voice—maybe a hint of regret or sadness—that made Kinsley want to ask questions. But she could feel Marcus's presence like the first rays of sunlight after a storm. She didn't want to discuss family matters in front of him. They were too complicated, and even she couldn't wrap her head around what had happened and all she had lost.

"You have a wonderful life now," she reminded Elizabeth.

"I do, but I worry about you. I don't want you getting hurt. I know you want to find your father's killer, but I'm worried that you're putting yourself in danger. There is a killer on the loose, Kins. What if he comes after you?"

They'd had the same conversation several times before.

Kinsley didn't want to have it again.

"I'm being careful. I promise. Look, I don't want to rush away, Elizabeth, but I'm with a friend."

"A friend? Male or female?"

"Does it matter?"

"So, male. Interesting. I'll expect the details when I call next. Much love, hon." She disconnected.

Kinsley finally met Marcus's eyes.

"Sorry about that," she murmured, tucking the phone into her bag and grabbing her coat from a peg near the door.

"Why?"

"It's late. I'm sure you're anxious to get me back to the apartment so you can get on with your night. Did you find anything there?"

"Nothing. We did speak to the neighbor. He insisted he saw someone walking to the rear of the house. Charlotte accessed the security footage, but all we were able to see was a dark shadow. No clear details. Whoever it was, was there and left. It's possible it was just a curious passerby. Charlotte does have an impressive property."

"Possible? But not likely?"

"I'm not sure, but your apartment is secure. No one was near it."

"Then you can take me home and get me out of your hair," she said, only half-joking. "I'm sure you have plenty of other things you could be doing besides sitting here with me."

"My night was supposed to be devoted to getting to know you. I have no other plans," he responded as he stared into her eyes, made her feel as if she were the only important thing in his world.

It had to be a trick, a tactic used by police officers everywhere, but she was pulled into and toward him in a way she hadn't expected. "You're a sweet talker, Marcus."

"A truth teller." He helped her into her coat. "I'm sorry I was gone for so long."

"I understand. My dad had long days and nights. But that made the time we had together even more special."

"You never resented him for being away?"

"No. He was a great dad. He was involved in my life. He knew my friends and my interests. He asked me questions about things that mattered to me, and I always felt like he cared. So it never seemed like his job was more important. It just seemed like something he had to do, something he was passionate about, but not something that impacted our relationship."

"That's good to know."

"You're worried about Rosie?"

"She's already been through a lot. I don't want her to be hurt more," he said as they walked outside together. The clear sky had given way to thick clouds. A few flurries drifted across the grayed blackness.

"Rosie is going to be fine," she assured him,

because she believed it. A child who was loved, thrived—and Rosie was very well loved.

"I hope so. I go to sleep every night praying that she will be. I wake up every morning and do the same. My parents' deaths had a huge impact on Jordyn. That's the only way I can explain the path she took. I don't want Rosie walking the same one."

"You can't assume she'll make the same mistakes as her mother," Kinsley offered. "The prosecutors brought up my mother a lot during my trial. She was an alcoholic and addicted to pain medication. She'd left me and my dad when I was three. The way they painted things, I was my mother's daughter, partying hard and not caring about the people I hurt. Elizabeth said they were putting a giant question mark on my character because of a person who hadn't been in my life for over a decade. As if genetics determines fate. It doesn't."

"That must have been hard on you," he said as he held open the SUV door.

"The entire thing was hard. Hearing about my mother's sins and my supposed repeat of them, being accused of a heinous crime that I did not commit. No part of that was easy." She slid into the vehicle, pulling her coat a little tighter against the chill. "But none of that compared to finding my father dead."

"I can't imagine what that was like," he said.

She was close enough to see hints of green and gold in his eyes. She looked away, surprised at herself for noticing.

"You lost your parents at a young age," she stated, quickly changing the subject.

"I was eleven."

"So, you do know what that's like," she affirmed, keeping her attention focused on the front window as he closed her door and walked to the other side of the vehicle.

Kinsley shouldn't be feeling the way she was—hyperaware of Marcus and a little off balance because of him. She wasn't naive enough to think she was simply tired or overly emotional after talking to her uncle. She knew what she was feeling, and she knew it was different than the way she'd felt when she'd met her high school boyfriend. She'd been a child then, feeling grown up because she could drive and because all the little-kid rules no longer applied to the older teenager she was becoming.

But she had still been a child.

She hadn't understood the kind of commitment and care it took to stand by someone through long years and hardships. She'd had no concept of what a lasting relationship would require. Prison and time had changed her perspective.

She knew that what she was feeling for Marcus wasn't a quick blush of giddy teen attraction. It was the real deal, a deep-heart acknowledgment of his kindness, understanding and honesty.

Those were characteristics that didn't change.

Those were attributes that remained when looks and strength faded.

"You're quiet," Marcus said as he pulled out of his driveway and onto the road. Clouds had rolled in, covering the nearly full moon. The world seemed cast in a yellow-gray hue that turned the trees to burnished statues and grass into fields of molten gold.

"Just thinking."

"About the past."

"And the present," she replied. She wouldn't tell him that she had been thinking about him. That her mind had been working through what her heart had already discovered.

He was a man worthy of notice, one she would like to spend more time with.

"About your father's case?"

"Yes. If his murderer is after me, he's not hiding like he was while I was in prison. His presence here is proof that he is willing to take risks. As long as I'm accessible to him, he'll continue to do so, and that means the chances of him making a mistake and getting caught are high."

"What do you mean by 'accessible'?" Marcus's voice had gone hard, the edginess making her muscles tense. She recognized the sound of a police officer readying an explanation for how things were going to be.

"Out of prison. Not locked up. Moving through the world and causing him more trouble than he's had since he shot my father."

"I hope you're not thinking of yourself as bait," he nearly growled.

"I wasn't, but *bait* is as good a word as any."

"Good word. Terrible idea."

"Someone needs to draw him out. The police can't or won't. No one else has the power to make him sweat the way I do."

"The police do, and they can."

"Come on, Marcus. You know the truth. My father's case is nearly two decades old. It's about as cold as any case can get."

"There are new DNA tests and the potential that the perp who left DNA on the cup on your father's coffee table is in the system now."

"It's been checked and rechecked. I pushed until I was certain they ran everything again when I was released." There were no matches in the database. If the perpetrator was arrested and swabbed, he'd be linked with her father's murder. The police in Miami were content to rely on that happening. Kinsley was not.

"I've spoken to the Miami police. The guy in charge of your father's case is doing the footwork, reinterviewing witnesses and gathering new information."

"New information? From what he's told me, there isn't any."

"He is attempting to get new information," he corrected. "As you know, it's a cold case, getting it to heat back up again is challenging."

"Apparently, my hiring a private investigator to dig into things is doing that. Until then, things were quiet around here," she pointed out.

Kinsley hadn't hired the investigator to bring the perp out of the woodwork. She'd done it because she'd been worried the police would be limited in their methods or wouldn't care enough to ask tough questions of reputable people.

"Right, and I'd like them to quiet down again. Frenchtown isn't a trap, and you aren't the bait that has been placed to draw a predator in." He reiterated his point.

"I didn't miss your point the first time you made it," she said. "And my point remains the same. If he's going to come after me, we may as well use it to our advantage."

Marcus's jaw tightened. "*We* are not doing anything that involves investigating a criminal case."

"That's fine. I've been going it alone for a

long time. Being part of a team isn't necessary to my success," she responded, purposely mis-understanding him.

His lips quirked in a half smile and he shook his head. "You know what I meant."

"You know I can't stop, Marcus. You wouldn't. Not if it were your father."

"And fifteen years of my life spent behind bars? You're right. I wouldn't." He pulled up to the only stop sign between his place and town, his hands loose on the steering wheel. "I want you safe, Kinsley. That is my top priority."

"And mine is to find my father's killer."

"If I ask why you're prioritizing that, will you answer?" He glanced in the rearview mir-ror, then pulled into the intersection and took a hard left onto a narrow road.

"Are you taking me for a ride until I do?" she asked, more surprised than concerned.

"Just making sure we're not being followed," he responded.

"Followed?" She glanced back and saw a car moving through the intersection.

"He's been behind us almost since I pulled out of my driveway. Came out of nowhere and has been keeping a steady distance."

The road ended abruptly, asphalt giving way to dirt and grass. In the distance, a lake spread like a black stain across the landscape.

"Old Man's Wish," Marcus said as he executed a three-point turn.

"What's that?"

"The lake. It's called Old Man's Wish. At least, that's what people in town have always called it."

"Why?"

"That's a story for next week's dinner," he responded.

"Next week?"

"Neighbors have dinner once a week around here."

"They do not," she responded. But she laughed, because he was funny and sweet, and when she was with him, she could almost forget that she'd spent most of her adult life in prison.

"Maybe not, but it's a tradition we should start. Don't you think?" He had the SUV turned toward the main road, the engine idling, trees to both sides, the cloud-thick sky above. They could have been the only two people in the world.

For a moment, it felt like they were. It felt like they had always known each other and that this evening was one of dozens that had come before it. Kinsley didn't feel uncomfortable around Marcus. She didn't feel gauche, uncertain or inexperienced, either. She had been out with two men since her release. Both were people Elizabeth had known. Both times, the evening had ended with Kinsley feeling uncultured and socially inept.

With Marcus, there was no pressure to be anything other than herself.

"Yes, I think so."

"You're not sure?"

"I'm not great in social situations. If you haven't noticed."

"I haven't." He looked into her eyes, studying her face as if she were a mystery he was trying to solve.

"Well, that's good. I guess I'm doing better than I was a couple years ago."

"A couple of years ago, you'd just been released. You'd lived your entire adult life inside prison walls. You've had almost three years to grow," he reminded her. "And, for the record, you're doing great."

"At what?"

"Adjusting to life outside. It's not easy. I know plenty of people who are released and end up back in." He accelerated then stepped so hard on the brake, she flew forward. The seat belt caught her before she hit the dash.

"What's wrong?" she said.

"Get out of the car." He barked the order and she obeyed, opening the door and jumping out as he did the same.

He grabbed her hand and pulled her off the road.

"What's going on?" she asked as he led her farther from the vehicle.

"Someone is coming."

"Where?" She glanced back and saw head-lights gleaming on asphalt.

They weren't just coming, they were there.

A dark SUV, hood gleaming, tires gliding almost noiselessly over the pavement. It looked exactly like the vehicle that had pulled over the night she had nearly been kidnapped.

"That's it," she said breathlessly as Marcus dragged her deeper into the woods.

"What?" he whispered, his lips so close to her ear, she could feel the warmth of his breath on her skin.

"The SUV. It's the same one that was on the road the night I was nearly kidnapped," she replied, her voice shaky, her body humming with adrenaline.

She wanted to head back to the SUV and get a photo of the license plate and the occupant.

"You're sure? There are lots of dark SUVs out there," Marcus said, not slowing his pace.

She'd lost sight of the road and the vehicle, but she was as certain as she could be. "As sure as I can be. It was a dark-colored SUV. Same size. Same shape. I want to see if the driver is the same. Then I'll know for sure." She tried to tug away, but he had a firm grip on her hand and didn't seem inclined to release it.

"*I'm* going back," he said, stopping near an old tree that had uprooted and left a deep crevice. "You're going to stay hidden until I tell you it's safe."

"That's not a good idea," she argued. "I know what—"

"Kinsley, see that hole?" He pointed to the area beneath the tree's massive root system. "I want you to climb down in there. I'm texting an on-duty officer to provide some backup. I'll send him your coordinates."

"But—"

"The longer we waste arguing, the more likely it is that we're going to be discovered or that I'm going to miss an opportunity to talk to our only other person of interest."

Kinsley swallowed another protest and did what he'd told her to do, sliding down the steep side of the hole, bits of tree root and rock snagging her clothing and scratching her skin.

"Kinsley?" Marcus said quietly.

She looked up.

He was on his belly, half his torso hanging inside the pit. "Stay here until Sergeant Ford or I come to get you. Promise me, you will."

She looked into his eyes, saw the concern in his face, and said the only thing she could.

"I will."

* * *

Marcus eased through sparse undergrowth, belly to the ground, staying low because winter foliage didn't offer much cover. He had known the moment he'd seen the other vehicle in his rearview mirror that trouble was coming. He'd felt it in his gut the same way he had when he'd been a soldier moving through enemy territory.

Still, he'd been hoping he was wrong.

The escalation of attacks was alarming, and leaving Kinsley in a hole in the ground, hiding from someone who wanted her dead, didn't fill him with good cheer. She deserved more than this. She deserved peace and as much happiness as she could find.

A car door closed, the sound setting off alarm bells in his head. People didn't come down this road at night. They rarely came down it during the day. Locals knew it dead-ended at the lake and that it was private property. The No Trespassing signs hanging in the trees shouted it to strangers. If a person didn't know the lake was there, they'd never see it at night.

He eased between evergreens, the scent of needles drifting around him. The air was cold, the ground nearly frozen. If something happened to him, Kinsley would be okay. As long as she stayed where she was. The hole was large and deep enough to conceal her from anyone hunting on foot. Her heat signature would be hidden by the cold ground and frozen root systems that shrouded her.

If she stayed there.

He could imagine her crawling out, right into the sites of a killer.

Dry leaves crunched as someone walked across the pavement.

Marcus inched forward, trying to get a look at the license plate and the person. He'd already texted Tyree Ford. Once the squad car pulled in, the suspect would be unable to flee by vehicle.

Leaves rustled as someone stepped into the trees a few feet away. The moon was full but hidden behind thick clouds. Marcus could see the man's height and shape, light hair under a dark ball cap. The details of his face were veiled in shadows, but the firearm in his hand was clearly visible. It looked like a Glock, a sound suppressor on the muzzle.

He had obviously entered the woods to commit murder. And it looked like he didn't plan to leave until he'd accomplished his goal.

Was he the man who had murdered Kinsley's father?

The sound of tires on asphalt broke through the quiet. Tyree Ford was on his way. Sirens and lights off—just the way he should approach an unknown situation. Marcus had warned him of the potential for an armed and dangerous perp. A military veteran who'd served in Iraq, Ford had been an officer in LA before he'd moved to Montana to be closer to his wife's family. She'd passed away from cancer a few years later, and he'd stayed to raise their twin daughters close to family.

Tyree Ford hadn't survived the brutality of war to die on a quiet road outside a small town.

Marcus hadn't brought his firearm. When he was off-duty, it stayed locked in the gun safe. He did have surprise on his side. He moved quietly, easing into an upright position, his eyes fixed on the gunman. The man was tense, his hand tight around the gun, his movements brittle and sharp, as if he were close to his breaking point.

One noise and he'd fire.

One hint that someone was on to him and he'd pull the trigger without thinking or caring about the consequences. He was a loose cannon. Marcus couldn't afford to let him go off.

The sound of tires ceased, the hum of the cruiser carrying into the trees. A door opened and leaves crackled underfoot. Tyree was heading into the trees, following the coordinates Marcus had sent. He had no clue what he was walking into.

"Police!" Marcus called out, his voice breaking the silence and startling birds from a nearby tree.

The gunman swung in his direction, firing a round before he'd even seen his target, the quiet pop belying the deadliness of the projectile. The bullet went wild, whizzing through leaves as Marcus dove for cover. A bullet tore into the ground near his hand, bits of rock and earth flying into his face. He could hear Tyree radio for backup. It wouldn't be long and the Frenchtown police department would be responding in force.

"Frenchtown Police! Put your weapon down and show yourself!" Tyree yelled as the sound of sirens filled the air.

The perp took off, racing through the trees, gun still in hand.

Marcus followed. He wasn't going to let the guy slip through his fingers. "Police! Drop the weapon! Now!" he shouted.

The perp swung toward him, firing haphazardly. The bullet ricocheted off a pine tree, shrapnel slamming into Marcus's neck. Blood oozed from the wound, but he didn't have time to assess the damage.

He launched himself at the shooter, slamming into him and knocking him off his feet. They both went down, tangled in a thicket of brambles, fighting for control of the gun.

NINE

As a kid, Kinsley had known how to stand up for herself. She hadn't been a fighter, but she hadn't been passive, either. Her father had wanted her to be tough and kind in her dealings with other people. He had taught her the fine art of communication and the importance of picking her battles.

Prison had taught her to be quiet, to keep her own counsel, and to obey. She had been given a life sentence with possibility of parole after twenty-five years. She had tiptoed through each day, hoping to avoid trouble and to keep her record clean.

She had wanted out of prison not just because she had wanted her freedom but because she had wanted justice for herself and for her father.

It had taken her a while to realize that being released hadn't given her freedom. She was still in prison, her mind and body insisting she continue the habits she had learned when locked away. Solitude. Obedience. Silence.

She waited in the hole, back pressed to soft earth and spiky roots. The tree had left a craterlike area. She had crawled under the roots, hiding herself as deeply as she could. She imagined bugs crawling out of the dead wood and scurrying down her jacket. Or, worse, snakes slithering out of their winter slumber.

She shuddered.

How long had she been waiting? Fifteen minutes? Twenty? It felt like an eternity, and it felt like she should climb out of the hole and make certain Marcus was okay. She'd heard muffled shouts a few minutes ago. Since then, she'd heard nothing.

So she'd waited.

Just like she'd been told.

Her mind was screaming for her to crawl out and go to battle with him, but her gut was telling her that would cause more trouble.

The wind had picked up and bits of dirt and leaves were falling into the hole, coating her face and head with a layer of dust and debris. The soft moan of swaying trees and the whistle of wind between pine boughs was an eerie backdrop to the unnatural silence of the forest. There should be deer and elk browsing the undergrowth in search of succulent greenery.

Kinsley shifted and dirt rained down on her head. She hadn't realized how tightly she had squeezed herself into the root system of the tree. Her hair caught and more dirt fell, the soft thump of clods landing nearly covering the quieter sound of branches snapping.

Something—or someone—was coming.

She felt around the darkness, searching for a rock or a stick that she could use to defend herself. She tried not to imagine a man standing above her with a gun. She couldn't let her mind go to that place.

Her father had been shot eight times.

He had died almost instantly.

Her grandparents had taken comfort in that. Kinsley had not.

From that day forward, she had been terrified of guns.

The thought of dying from a gunshot horrified her, but not nearly as much as the thought of finding Marcus dead from one.

Or dying from one.

Bleeding and struggling.

She shuddered, her fingers curving around a fist-size rock. It wasn't much, but it was something.

The sounds drew closer, then stopped.

Dirt showered down on her head again, and she knew someone was above her. She didn't want to look up. She didn't want to see the monster from her nightmares staring down at her, gun in hand, ready to take her life and walk away.

Just the way he had with her father.

"Kinsley?" Marcus said quietly.

She screamed, the rock flying from her hand but falling short of the rim of the hole and his dark figure.

"Marcus!" she practically shouted, fear and relief making it difficult to modulate her voice. "What happened? Are you okay?"

She tried to climb up the dirt wall, but slid back, her hands scrabbling for something to hold on to.

He grabbed her wrist, pulling her up and over the edge.

"I was going to ask you the same thing," he commented.

"Nothing happened. I stayed low. Like you asked me to."

"I meant 'are you okay'?" he said.

Even with darkness shrouding his expression, Kinsley could see his smile, the lines deepening near his eyes.

The blood on his neck, his collar. Splattered on his light shirt.

"What happened?" she cried, turning on her phone's flashlight app to illuminate his face.

Marcus blinked and scowled. "Aside from the fact that you just blinded me, you mean?"

"Sorry." She turned the light away, flicking it off so that they were in the grayish darkness again. "You're bleeding."

"I was hit by shrapnel. It's nothing serious."

"It looks serious." She shrugged out of her coat and tried to press the sleeve against his neck. Her hands were shaking, and she dropped it instead.

Marcus picked it up and draped it around her shoulders.

"Kinsley, I'm fine," he said gently.

"You don't look fine." Her voice broke, fear making her weak.

"It's a lot of blood, but it's not enough to worry about. We need to get back to the SUV. I want to take you home and then get to the station."

"Did you catch the guy?"

"Yes." His hand curled around her upper arm as he shepherded her through the woods. Animals rustled in the undergrowth and then stilled as they walked by.

"And?"

"I had an officer take him to the station. We'll see if he plans to talk," he said as they stepped out of the woods and onto the road. The lake to their left gleamed silver-black in the darkness.

Spring would arrive soon. One season slipping into another. Kinsley had hoped this would be the year her father's killer would finally be found. She had prayed about it until the words stopped coming and only feelings remained. Desperation and longing. The fear that it would never happen.

Maybe this was the answer to all those prayers. The break she had been waiting for. She had paid the PI firm thousands of dollars. She'd pored through hundreds of documents, made dozens of calls, begged for help from the police… Had her time and effort come to nothing? She had no more idea now of who had murdered her father than she'd had during those long years in prison.

But then, her father's death had never made sense to her.

He hadn't been the kind of person to make enemies. His list of friends had spanned decades and encompassed every race, ethnicity and age. She had always assumed it had been someone he had arrested. Maybe a hit put out by someone involved in a crime he was investigating, but there had been no evidence. The FBI and Miami police had thoroughly investigated that angle.

They had come up empty.

"You're quiet," Marcus said as he opened the

door to his SUV. Another SUV was parked over to the side of the road, several officers dressed in white hazmat suits dusting it for prints and collecting evidence.

"Just thinking."

"About?"

"How long I've been waiting for answers and how hard it's been to find them."

"We're getting closer," he assured her.

"I know, but I don't want to get my hopes up."

"There's nothing wrong with hope." He closed her door and walked around to the driver's side of the car, sliding in and starting the engine.

Kinsley had expected him to be distracted by the activity that surrounded them—police cars and a CSI van, officers gathered beside the road—but he was focused on her. Hands lax on the wheel, blood splattered across his shirt and cheeks, his calmness was a sharp contrast to the electrified energy of the crime scene.

"There is when it comes to nothing."

"It never comes to nothing. If all it does is give a person the will to take one more step and go one more day and survive for another minute, then it has accomplished its goal. Don't you think?" He pulled forward, tires rolling along the pavement, leaves brushing the hood and sides as he maneuvered around people and vehicles.

"I've never thought about it that way, but you're right. It has."

Marcus smiled. "Did I just hear you say that I'm right?"

"You did hear me say it," she responded. "But I won't repeat it."

His laughter filled the vehicle and seemed to lodge itself deep in the darkest, loneliest part of her heart.

Kinsley had never imagined herself being comfortable around a person who worked for law enforcement. She had never thought it would even be possible. She had too many hard memories, and too many painful ones, but when she was with Marcus she forgot what he did for a living. All she knew was who he was as a person.

She studied his profile as he pulled onto the main road, not caring that he knew it. She didn't know how to play games. If she did, she wouldn't want to. "What happened out there?" she asked, reaching to pull his coat collar away from his neck. A deep gash ran across the side of it. Blood had dripped down onto his shirt, most of it dried and dark.

"He had a gun with a silencer. Not something he is going to be able to explain away very easily."

"Explain?"

"You know how it goes. *'I was out hunting. I thought I was shooting at a deer.'*"

She didn't, but she could imagine all those excuses being used. "It isn't hunting season," she noted.

"Poaching is a lot less of a punishment than first degree murder." He slowed as they reached town limits. The businesses were closed and dark, most people home and tucked into bed for the night. It wasn't a high-energy town, and it certainly wasn't the kind of place Kinsley had ever wanted to be.

But, she had learned to love the quiet pace of life.

She had learned to embrace solitude and quiet.

After so many years of sharing a cell and always having someone nearby, she was happy to have space and privacy.

"What are you thinking about?" Marcus asked as he pulled into Charlotte's driveway.

"That this place has grown on me, and that I'll be sad when I leave it."

"Why would you leave?"

"Once Doris retires, I won't have any reason to stay."

"You said it's grown on you, and you'll be sad to leave," he reminded her. "So why do you have to leave?"

"I...don't know."

"Maybe you should think about it. It would be a shame to give up something you like for no good reason."

Or for no reason at all.

He got out of the SUV, leaving it idling as he walked around to her side. He was taller than she was by nearly a foot, his shoulders broad, his arms and legs muscular. She should have found him intimidating. She didn't, and she couldn't put her finger on why she did not.

She had been around empathetic cops.

She had been around men who had treated her with respect and dignity.

But she had never once wanted to stay around them. She'd always wanted to run. If she couldn't, she'd felt trapped.

With Marcus, none of those feelings were there.

He walked her to the door and waited while she opened it.

When she would have stepped inside, he touched her arm. "Lock the door. Bolt it. Don't let anyone in, and don't come out until I call and tell you it's clear. If someone hired this guy, they're going to be waiting for a phone call. When it doesn't come, they might decide to finish the job themselves."

"I can't stay inside forever," she said.

"It won't take me forever to call." He cupped her jaw, his palm warm and a little rough. "I don't want to be worrying about you while I'm interviewing the suspect. Our resources are limited, and I can't pull an officer off the scene to stand guard here." The concern in his eyes was obvious, the faint frown line between his brows deepening with the weight of his concern.

"I'll stay here until I hear from you."

"Thanks." He smiled, the tension easing from his face. "I'm hoping the guy will spill everything."

"But?"

"That's not usually how it works. If he thinks he can weasel his way out of charges and time, he's not going to talk. It may be a long night. I'll update you as soon as I can." He dropped a kiss on her lips. A quick, light peck that could have been between two good friends if it hadn't felt like so much more.

Marcus seemed as surprised by it as she was, the small frown line deepening once again as he stared into her eyes. "I should apologize."

"But?" she asked. She didn't know what else to say. It had been too many years, and she'd had too little experience. She had no idea how to act around a man who might be interested in being more than friends.

"I'm not sorry. You're a beautiful woman,

Kinsley. When this is over, I'd like to spend more time with you… For now, I need to go. The longer the suspect thinks about things, the more time he has to make up stories. I'll call as soon as I have an update."

She should tell him that she wanted to spend more time with him, too. That would be the appropriate response.

Wouldn't it?

She didn't know.

And that bothered her a lot more than she wanted it to. She hated wasting energy on regrets and sorrows. She had her freedom. She needed to embrace it.

But she felt frozen by her insecurities.

"Be careful," she said, stepping inside.

"Lock the door," he responded as he jogged down the stairs.

She could have called out to him and said the words that were on the tip of her tongue, but he had work to do.

"Chicken," she muttered as she closed the door and let him walk away.

After four hours of questioning the man who'd shot at him, Marcus was no closer to getting answers.

He wanted the man who'd killed Michael King to be found and thrown in jail. Twenty years was a long escape from lawfulness. Marcus would feel blessed to be part of justice served.

He studied the perp through the one-way window, watching as he leaned back in a chair and stared up at the ceiling. Andrew Wright seemed unfazed by his arrest and had been sticking closely to his story. He was an out-of-work businessman from Florida, making his way across country, camping in backcountry areas, foraging for food and trying to stay off the grid. His story included seeing a deer cross the road and heading into the woods to find it.

The story hadn't been convincing, but his delivery had been Oscar-worthy.

The hotel key they'd found in his pocket seemed to disprove his story about camping out.

"What do you think?" Tyree asked. He was standing a few feet away, shoulder against the wall, hands shoved deep in his pockets. His shift had ended an hour ago, but he'd stuck around, hoping to see a turn in the tide.

"I think he has a lot riding on his ability to keep up the act," Marcus said, adjusting the collar of his dress shirt. He'd had to change out of the bloody one and into the only things he kept at the office. The shirt felt starched and uncomfortable, the crease in his pants too sharp for a small police department in a little town on the edge of nowhere.

"The background check was clean. No criminal record. Could he be telling the truth?" Tyree asked, his gaze shifting to the one-way and the man sitting alone in the room on the other side of it.

"No." Marcus gave a succinct answer. He didn't feel a need to explain or to justify. They'd worked together for nearly a decade; knew one another's modus operandi when it came to interrogations

"Making assumptions is a good way to limit possibilities."

"Do you think we're making assumptions?" Marcus turned his attention to Tyree, trying to read his expression. They'd been friends for years. They knew each other as cops, as hunting buddies. They were as close as brothers. If the sergeant had his doubts, Marcus would be wise to pay attention to them.

"No, but I'd like to search the hotel room he has in Missoula. That's a better use of your time. We can push him for answers all we want, but he's not going to budge. If we can get a warrant, we can get that done."

He was right. Andrew Wright might have a clean criminal record, but he also had the slickness of someone who'd been manipulating the system for years.

"Let's book him for assaulting an officer. He can argue his case to a judge. In the meantime, we'll see if things in town calm down once he's off the street."

"Things?" Tyree challenged. "Seems to me everything that is happening centers around Kinsley. She's brought a lot of trouble to town."

"That's not her fault. She was trying to get away from her past. She wasn't expecting it to follow her."

"No need to defend her. I'm not blaming her for what happened. I'm just making a statement about the results. I'll secure our perp. Then we can drive to the hotel. My kids have piano lessons this morning. If they miss another one, their teacher will kick them out. That is something neither will forgive me for, so let's get this show on the road."

Marcus waited in the open doorway as Tyree cuffed Wright and marched him out of the interrogation room.

For someone who had no criminal record, Wright seemed well rehearsed in the criminal justice system. He demanded an attorney immediately and seemed to expect to be released on bond shortly. Fortunately, small towns didn't have built-in public defenders. It would take a few hours to get one. Longer than that for the attorney to start moving toward a bond hearing. By that time, Marcus and Tyree would have the search warrant for Wright's hotel room. If there was anything there of use, they'd find it.

He hoped that would be the case.

The sooner Wright was permanently off the street, the better. Not only would the town be safer, so would Kinsley. He was as invested in that as he had ever been in anything. Her safety mattered. For professional reasons.

And for personal ones.

Marcus could allow himself to feel that way and to own it.

But, for now, he couldn't act on it.

The kiss had been a fluke. He wouldn't apologize. He wouldn't regret it. But he had no intention of repeating it.

Not now.

Not yet.

His focus had to be on justice, on safety, and on helping her find the person who had killed her father.

TEN

True to his word, Marcus kept Kinsley updated on the arrest of Andrew Wright. He'd asked her to come to the station to look at a lineup to try to identify the person she had seen the night she'd nearly been kidnapped.

She'd tried, but she hadn't been able to say with one-hundred-percent certainty. It had been too dark that night and the person had been too far away.

She'd felt like a failure, of course.

She had been desperate for answers and hopeful that she could identify the person.

She'd driven away feeling defeated.

"All I want is for life to be easy once in a while," she said, knowing Doris would hear and respond. They'd been working together for nearly three years. They'd talked about almost everything, but they'd never discussed Kinsley's past. They didn't talk about the night she had found her father, about the accusations, the conviction, the years she had spent in jail.

"Life is never easy, hon," Doris responded as she slid a pan of vanilla bean scones from the industrial-size oven at the back of the bakery.

"I'm very aware of that," Kinsley replied, trying to keep any hint of frustration out of her voice. Doris meant well, and she tried to be supportive, but platitudes were just that—platitudes. They meant nothing, changed nothing, and didn't help at all.

"I hope that didn't sound unfeeling. You know I care, and you know I understand how much you have been through."

"Yes. I do. You did a lot to help me, and I'll never forget that." Kinsley slid a tray of raspberry Danish onto a rack that would be wheeled out to the refrigerated display cases.

"I just don't want you to spend your life in limbo waiting for answers that you may or may not ever get."

"I'm going to get answers," she murmured, keeping her gaze lowered so that Doris couldn't read the frustration in her eyes. Too many people seemed to think that being released from prison was all she had needed to move forward with her life.

"Honey, your grandparents spent a fortune searching for answers. They paid a lot of really smart people a lot of really good money to find the same thing you're trying to find."

"That doesn't mean the answer can't be found. It just means it hasn't been."

Doris sighed the kind of long-suffering sigh Kinsley had always imagined a mother might use. "That's true."

"But?"

"There's nothing I can say that is going to steer you from the path you're on, so I won't try to make an argument for giving up on finding your father's killer and going on with your life. Just…be careful."

"I will be. I am. And you know that Charlotte's place has lots of security."

"I'm not just worried about your security. You're worn out. You work ten-or twelve-hour days. You never take time off."

"I don't need time off." And she had no idea what she would do if she had it. Sundays were for church, for laundry and for chores. Every other day of the week was filled with the bakery.

"Everyone needs time off. Your uncle is arriving this morning." It wasn't a question, but Kinsley nodded.

"He is."

"Don't you want to go to the airport to meet his plane?"

"He didn't give me the details, and I'm certain he doesn't expect me to do that."

"Expecting and wanting aren't the same. I spoke to Jay—"

"You spoke with Jay? When?" Kinsley was shocked. As far as she knew, Doris hadn't had contact with Jay since her grandmother's funeral. He had wanted nothing to do with anyone who'd supported Kinsley, and Doris hadn't seemed to want anything to do with him.

"Two days ago. He called me here. *Surprise* is a mild word for what I felt when he told me who he was."

"What did he want?"

"To apologize."

"For?"

"Not treating me like family the way his parents would have wanted. I was an aunt to those boys while they were growing up. Jay and Michael spent the night at my place every Saturday until your grandparents decided to move to Florida. The boys were ten. I visited three times a year until they graduated from high school." She smiled at the memories. "Needless to say, I told Jay he could stay with me when he's in town. He agreed but said he would take an Uber to my place."

"Is there a reason why you're just now telling me this?" Kinsley asked, surprised and a little alarmed that Doris was readily giving Jay a place to stay.

"I wasn't sure how to broach the subject. I know how you feel about your uncle."

"Then you know more than I do."

"This is a confusing time for all of us, but I want your family to mend its differences. It would make your grandparents happy, and I know your father would be heartbroken if he knew that you and Jay didn't speak to each another."

"That wasn't my choice, Doris," she said, trying to keep the anger out of her voice. Kinsley would have spoken to Jay, if he had ever reached out to her. During her years in prison, she had been desperate for connection with the outside world. She would have jumped at the opportunity to communicate with Jay. She had wanted that like she had wanted glimpses of daylight and the feel of cool, fresh air on her cheeks.

"I know, and you know my goal is only to see you happy."

"Right," Kinsley said, suddenly feeling constrained by the walls of the bakery, restricted by the closed door and the locked windows, and Doris's expectations that she would somehow be able to find happiness.

"So, take the day off. And, if you have it in you to, go pick your uncle up at the airport. He'd love that. This is his flight number and arrival time." She jotted both on a piece of paper and handed them to Kinsley.

Kinsley shoved it in her pocket and walked to the back door. She needed fresh air, and she didn't see any reason to stand around continuing to discuss things. "I *am* a little worn out. Maybe a day off isn't a bad idea," she said. "You're sure you have enough help?"

"Plenty. You go on home. Take a nap or go to the diner for breakfast. Do something for you for a change." Doris bustled away, already focused on the next batch of baked goods.

Kinsley grabbed her purse and coat from the hook near the door and walked outside.

She felt like a child sent to a time-out.

Only she hadn't done anything wrong, and she wasn't being punished. Her truck was parked near the back door as close to the building as she'd been able to manage. Even with Andrew Wright in jail, Kinsley didn't feel safe. She wasn't sure she ever would.

She climbed into the truck and pulled away from the bakery. It was Saturday morning, hours before dawn. Aside from the diner, nothing was open. There was no place to go and nothing to do. She could go back to the apartment, but even there she felt claustrophobic and trapped.

Until she could go where she wanted without worrying, she would never be free.

She drove through town, the sky untouched by the golden light of dawn. The businesses were dark, the streets empty. She passed Charlotte's place and continued on. She had no clear destination in mind, but she found herself outside of town, heading toward her house. She had left the cleanup and restoration to the professionals. There had been no major glitches, and if things continued that way, she'd be moving back in within a week.

She'd feel better then.

She'd feel more like herself and less like the prisoner she had once been. She passed Marcus's house. His cruiser was parked in the driveway, his SUV next to it.

She needed to be careful with him.

She'd begun to anticipate his phone calls. She'd begun to look forward to seeing him. Their friendship was blooming, and she could see it blossoming into something deeper.

Kinsley wasn't sure how she felt about that.

Or how she *should* feel.

She turned onto her street, surprised by the longing she felt as she reached the house. She hadn't meant to make this home. She certainly hadn't thought she would want to stay in such a cold climate and unfamiliar area. She had been

born and raised in Florida. She had spent her
teenage years swimming in the ocean and kay-
aking through the waterways. Her prison term
had also been spent in Florida. Locked away,
but able to go out into the yard and inhale the
familiar fragrance of her childhood memories.

Florida was heat and sun and humid air. The
dusky scent of damp earth and rain. The sweet
scent of hyacinth and honeysuckle.

Montana was ice and snow. Hot summer days
and cool summer nights. Mountain views and
pine trees. The lonely cry of the red-tailed hawk
and the sweet trill of the cardinal. Both places
were unique and lovely testaments to God's cre-
ative genius and His spectacular artistry. He
was a God of the sun and the moon, the summer and the winter. Through planting and sow-
ing. Through every season of life, He was. It
was good to remember that. To focus on God's
power rather than her weakness.

He was in charge.

Her grandmother had said that often. *He is
in charge. He has the power to change things.
He can and* will *do what He desires.*

There had been years when that had made
Kinsley angry. Years when she had needed
somewhere to focus her fury. God had been
the target of seething rage and sharp disappointment. Even then, He had stayed true. She had

made friends in prison. She'd forged relationships that had helped her navigate the terrifying unknowns. Eventually, anger had turned to acceptance and the unwavering desire to see justice done.

God had granted her freedom from what could have destroyed her. He had allowed her to turn away from hatred and unhappiness. She would always be grateful for that. She would always acknowledge the good He had done in her life. Despite all the bad, she had made it through.

She owed that to Him and to the love of the few people who had continued to believe in her.

Jay was not one of them.

The fact that he was arriving that afternoon and that Doris thought it would be a good idea for Kinsley to meet him at the airport and drive him to Doris's made her stomach churn.

She had been hurt too many times by too many people who had once claimed to love her. She didn't want to be hurt again.

If she went to the airport and Jay refused to speak to her or told her he didn't need or want a ride, she would be devastated. He had been like a second father. He was part of most of her best childhood memories. He was also in so many of her worst ones.

He was a replica of who her father would have

been had he lived, and she had no idea how she would feel when she saw him.

Kinsley got out of the truck and unlocked the front door, walking inside the house for the first time in several days. She flicked the light switch and was pleased when the entryway lights came on. The fire damage to the house had been minimal, but the smoke and water damage had been severe. Water remediation had been completed, and it looked like the contracting company had replaced all the wiring and the light fixtures. The drywall was up and spackled along the seams. Soon, they'd paint, and she'd be able to return.

A few days. A week. A blink of an eye compared to the time she had spent in prison. She walked into the kitchen and dropped her purse on the counter. Most of her furniture had to be replaced. The kitchen set, the living room furniture, her bedroom set.

A couple folding chairs leaned against the kitchen wall. She carried one into the living room. The fireplace had already been inspected. The old wood floor had dried and been refinished. She'd chosen a soft gray paint for the walls. A large tub of it was sitting in the middle of the floor, drop clothes folded neatly beside it. Aside from that, the room was empty. Most of her belongings, tossed into a rented dumpster, had been hauled away.

Not that she'd had much.

She'd salvaged a few family photos. A bin of photo albums had been untouched by the fire and protected by the deluge of water. The safe with her grandmother's jewelry and her father's watch was still in the closet in her room. His Bible was there, too. Notes written in tiny letters in the margins.

She'd spent hours poring over it, studying the sharp quick angle of his letters. Wondering if he'd left hidden messages there. But, her father had been a scholar. He'd put the same passion into studying the word of God as he had into getting his college degree. All his notes had been about the Bible passages he was reading. No messages for her, but she still treasured it.

Kinsley settled into the chair, listening to the creak and groan of the old house. The heater hummed quietly in the background, pumping warm air through the floor vents. Even without furniture, this felt more like home than any other place had in a very long time. If she let herself, she could imagine spending the rest of her life here. Creating a community of friends and neighbors. People who could count on her and on whom she could count. It was a nice fantasy. A couple years ago, she would have dismissed it as nothing more than that. Now, she wondered if she could make the fantasy a reality.

Someone knocked on the door, the sound so startling, she nearly fell out of her chair. She jumped up, hurrying to look out the peephole. Marcus stood on the porch. Her heart jumped in acknowledgment, her hands shaking as she unlocked and opened the door.

Silly to be so shaken by his presence.

Silly to be so happy to see him.

But she was both those things and, when he smiled, she couldn't help smiling in return.

"It's awfully early to be out and about," she said.

"I was letting Fitz out and I saw the light on at your place. I thought I'd check things out."

"You walked over?" she asked, grabbing another chair from the kitchen and motioning for him to sit.

"Yes." He looked tired, his face unshaved, his eyes shadowed.

"Want some coffee?"

"You have a way to make it?"

"No." Her cheeks heated, and he smiled again. "Didn't expect me to take you up on the offer?"

"Didn't think through the offer before I made it," she admitted.

"We can go out to get some," he suggested.

"The only place open this early is the diner."

"The Daily Grind makes a mean cup of coffee, if you don't mind a ride to Missoula."

"With you?" she asked.

"You did offer me coffee," he replied.

"I have to pick my uncle up at the airport this morning. We may have to get coffee another time," she said, her heart fluttering as she met his eyes. He had a way of watching her that made her feel beautiful and interesting and valued.

"I didn't realize that was on your agenda."

"It wasn't. It was on Doris's. She told me to take the day off so I could spend time with Jay."

"Sounds like we both have the day off. How about we go get some coffee, then get your uncle?" he suggested, standing and holding out his hand.

Kinsley knew what she shouldn't do. She shouldn't go to the coffee shop with him or allow him to accompany her to the airport.

She shouldn't count on his kindness.

But he *had* been kind, and it had been decades since her heart had fluttered when she'd looked into a man's eyes.

She took his hand and allowed him to pull her to her feet.

* * *

Marcus had watched enough video footage of the press conferences Jay King had participated in to know what he looked like. Tall. Dark hair. Glasses. A broad smile. There'd been news footage of him after Kinsley's release, angry and accusatory, his wife standing quietly beside him.

Neither had seemed willing to believe in Kinsley's innocence. Maybe Jay had finally changed his mind, but the visit seemed odd, the timing seemed off. Sure, Marcus had wanted to enjoy a cup of coffee with Kinsley, but he'd also wanted to make certain she didn't disappear after picking her uncle up from the airport.

He walked beside her as she made her way to baggage claim, watching the way she smoothed her bangs and adjusted her ponytail. She was nervous, her freckles dark against her pale skin.

"It's going to be okay," he said, touching her shoulder.

She seemed to lean toward him, as if she felt the invisible draw between them, the silky chord that seemed to pull a little tighter each time they were together. He hadn't wanted a relationship. Not now, with so many other things that needed his focus, but he couldn't deny his attraction to Kinsley. He would risk heartache to spend more time with her, to get to know her better, to help her find her way out of the past and into the present.

"I hope so," she said, her take-out coffee seemingly forgotten in her hand, the contents sloshing through the opening in the lid and dripping down the side.

"Want me to hold that?" he asked, taking it before she could respond.

"Thanks. I'm too nervous to drink it."

"It's been a while since you've seen him."

"The last time I actually saw him was at my sentencing hearing. He wasn't at the prison when I was released, and I wasn't surprised."

"Were you disappointed?"

"I didn't expect anyone to be there, so I wasn't disappointed."

"I'm sorry."

"You had nothing to do with it."

"I'm still sorry. It can't be easy to feel like everyone you know has turned his back on you."

"Feel like? Everyone did, Marcus, and I don't ever want to experience that again."

"Is that why you haven't made friends in town?"

"Who says I haven't?" she queried, her gaze on the arrival gate where a few people were beginning to appear.

"Observation. We've been neighbors for a few years."

"And you've observed that I don't have friends?" She raised a dark red brow, a hint of amusement in her eyes.

"I've noticed that you go to work and come home—on Repeat."

"I also attend church," she pointed out. "But, you're right. I've kept my distance. I only planned to be here until Doris sold Flour and Fancies. Making friends wasn't high on my priority list."

"I thought you'd moved to be closer to her," he said.

"I came because the bakery was struggling financially. Doris needed help. She wanted to retire, but the business wasn't profitable and she couldn't sell it. She was planning to close the doors, but I thought I could help her get it on a more steady financial footing. That way she could sell for a profit and move on."

"From what I've seen, you've accomplished that. The bakery is always packed."

"Sales are excellent. Doris is at a point where she can make decisions about her future."

"And you?"

"Me?" She finally met his eyes, her attention intense and focused.

"Where do you plan to go? When you leave?"

"I've been thinking about that," she replied, her eyes the color of the sky at twilight. "I like

Montana. I like Frenchtown. And, honestly, since I met you and your family, I feel like I have connections here. People who…care about me."

"Winnie and Rosie adore you," he said, and realized his mistake immediately.

Her eyes shuttered and she looked away.

"What I meant to say…" he began.

She tensed, took a step toward the arrival gate and stopped.

"That's Jay," she said, pointing to a tall, dark-haired man who was following a line of people, his attention focused on his phone. "That's what my father would have looked like. I can't even tell you how many times I thought about that in prison."

"About what?" Marcus asked gently, his focus on Jay King. The man he'd seen so many times in news footage from the original trial hadn't aged much. He was tall, dark-haired, and affable-looking. Clean-shaved, wire-rimmed glasses and business attire, he didn't look like someone with a vendetta, but that didn't mean he wasn't responsible for the attacks on Kinsley. With Wright's silence continuing, there had been no new leads on the case and no further attacks.

Marcus wanted to believe that Wright, for reasons of his own, had targeted Kinsley. If that were the case, his arrest and incarceration would keep her safe.

He didn't believe it.

He had been in law enforcement for a long time. He knew that a person acted in the heat of passion or was motivated by circumstance. Generally, those were financial or emotional. Someone had to have something to gain or something to lose to commit a crime.

Wright had no connection to Kinsley.

He had no relationship with anyone in her family.

His motivation *had* to be financial.

Someone was paying him. If they could find out who, they could stop the attacks against Kinsley and find her father's murderer.

"I guess I need to tell him we're here," Kinsley said. "It's been so long, he's probably forgotten what I look like."

"It would be really hard to forget your hair and eyes," Marcus responded.

Her cheeks flushed, but she didn't respond. Her focus was on her uncle.

He'd looked up from his phone and was scanning the area.

When he saw her, he smiled and picked up his pace, tucking the phone into his pocket.

"Kinsley! It's been a long time!" He opened his arms as if to embrace her.

Kinsley stepped back, nearly bumping into Marcus.

His arm slid around her waist, his fingers resting lightly on her rib cage, the gesture unconscious and driven by the need to offer support and protection.

"That wasn't my choice," she responded.

"No, it was mine. I was wrong, and I'm sorry." Jay pushed his glasses up as he stared unflinchingly into Kinsley's eyes.

"Right." She looked away first, her gaze shifting to a family that was passing by. "This isn't the time or the place to discuss that. Doris asked me to pick you up."

"Doris told me you wanted to be here. She didn't say you had to be coerced into coming." Jay's smile faded.

"I wasn't coerced," Kinsley said. "I agreed to come."

She seemed to be trying to move the conversation and the meeting along as quickly as possible.

Jay's expression tightened but he nodded. "Right. For Doris."

"Does it matter why?" Her tone was sharp, her gaze wary.

"To me? Yes. It does. When Doris told me you were coming, I thought..." He shook his head. "Obviously, what I thought doesn't matter. If it makes you uncomfortable to ride to Doris's with me, I'll be happy to get an Uber."

"It's fine. Marcus and I are already here. Do you have luggage?"

"Just the carry-on. I'm only here for a few days." He shifted his gaze to Marcus. "You're Chief Bayne."

It wasn't a question, but Marcus nodded. "Marcus."

"Nice to meet you." Jay offered a quick, firm handshake. "I was hoping to speak with you while I was here."

"I was hoping for the same. If it'll make it easier, we can talk on the way to Doris's." Marcus started moving, his arm still around Kinsley as they walked out of the airport and into the overcast morning.

"I don't mind going to your office," Jay said, his gaze shifting to Kinsley.

Whatever he had to say, he didn't want her to hear it.

"If you don't want me privy to the conversation, I can Uber home," Kinsley said stiffly, her cheeks still red, her hands fisted. She was obviously uncomfortable and angry.

Marcus couldn't blame her.

He'd watched the news footage. He knew what Jay had said during and after the trial.

There had been no love for his niece. No compassion. Certainly, no grace.

Had that changed?

Or was this an act designed to lower her guard?

"It isn't that, Kinsley," Jay said, his long stride shortened to match Kinsley's.

"Then, what is it?"

"You've been through enough. I don't want to put you through more."

"By doing what? Telling the police that you think I'm guilty of my father's murder?"

"I don't believe you're guilty," Jay responded, his face a little pale.

"You're about twenty years too late for that." Her voice was even. No anger. No recrimination. Just a statement of fact.

"We have a lot to discuss." Jay cleared his throat. "And I have a lot to make up for. How about, for now, I just tell you I'm sorry again?"

Kinsley nodded stiffly.

She had been hurt more than anyone should be.

She had lost decades of her life and nearly everyone she loved. She had a right to her defensiveness and to the fear Marcus glimpsed in her eyes as she slid into his SUV.

He leaned closer to her as Jay climbed into

the back seat, his lips brushing her ear. "It's going to be okay."

She nodded but wouldn't meet his eyes as he closed the door and rounded the vehicle. He would drop Jay off at Doris's house. He'd meet with the guy and listen to what he had to say, but what he would never understand is how someone who had claimed to love Kinsley, who had spent hours with her as she'd grown and matured, could ever have thought she was responsible for her father's death.

Anger often came with defensiveness.

Marcus had heard plenty of felons argue virulently for their freedom. Most willingly threw friends and relatives under the bus to turn police attention in other directions. In her taped police interviews, Kinsley had looked and sounded despondent. She'd been visibly crying, her face streaked with mascara left over from her night of partying. When asked who would want to harm her father, she had said he had no enemies. When pressed, she'd suggested they look at her father's recent cases.

Even then, she'd been intelligent, running through options, discarding most. A convict with a vendetta had made the most sense. The fact that she had been able to reason it through in the middle of the devastation of losing her father had been used against her. Prosecuting attorneys had claimed she had planned the shooting and made it look like a hit, hoping the police would suspect someone her father had arrested. With the evidence they'd gathered at the scene, including her fingerprints and DNA, they were able to convince a jury of her peers.

They had been proved wrong.

And, while the circus-like trial had progressed, two people who were closest to Michael King had been totally ignored by the police. Jay, and Michael's then fiancée, Elizabeth Harvey.

Both had seemed to skate under law enforcement radar.

They'd had alibies. But alibies could be faked.

The police had found a viable suspect in Kinsley, and from what Marcus had seen of the case files, they had turned most of their attention in that direction.

Had Jay used his supposed grief and righteous rage to hide the truth? Had he purposely shifted police focus to his niece?

Was he guilty of more than not believing in Kinsley's innocence?

Was he capable of killing his brother?

Or of having someone do it?

Those were questions Marcus needed answers to.

The way he saw things, Jay was the only person besides Kinsley who'd stood to gain from Michael's death. If money was the motive, Jay was the prime suspect.

If love or lust was, Elizabeth Harvey might be at the top of the list. It was something he had been thinking about as he'd poured over the case files and evidence. He hadn't mentioned it to Kinsley. Not yet. She had enough on her mind without him hinting that one of the few people who had stood beside her during her trial had actually been guilty of the crime.

Until he had more proof, he was keeping quiet.

Eventually, he would broach the subject and get Kinsley's thoughts.

He wanted to find the truth.

He just hoped that when he did, Kinsley would have the peace she so desperately seemed to need.

ELEVEN

The ride to Doris's house was less awkward
than Kinsley had anticipated. She'd imagined
stilted small talk about the weather, but Marcus asked Jay about his family—a wife Kinsley had never met and two children that were in
their middle teens. Jay regaled them with stories about the farmstead he'd bought in Penn-
sylvania, the goats his kids had begged for that
continually escaped their pen, and a young
sheepdog named Fred who let them wander the
yard while he lazed in the sun.

The life he described was idyllic. The picture
he painted of his family one that anyone would
have longed for.

A few years ago, Kinsley would have been
angry about the unfairness of it. That someone
who had been so mistaken—who had treated
her so wrongly—could be so blessed, seemed
unjust.

The truth was that she had never wanted

Jay to suffer. She had always wanted her uncle happy. He had lost his only sibling and his closet friend. His fury before, during and after the trial was more understandable than her having resentment over his good fortune.

"I'd invite you both in, but it's Doris's place, and I don't want to be presumptuous," Jay said as they pulled up in front of Doris's quaint two-story cottage.

Kinsley could have told him that Doris wouldn't mind him offering the invitation, but she wanted some time to think about this first meeting. The transition from not speaking at all to suddenly talking freely had been seamless.

She had expected worse.

She *always* expected worse.

Maybe this was God's way of telling her that she shouldn't. Maybe He was showing her that good things happened, that life had a bright side, that the worst thing wasn't always what she would get.

Kinsley needed to think about that.

She needed to accept the dull ache of loss she felt when she looked in Jay's eyes. When she saw her father in his face and remembered, all over again, that she would never speak to him again, never hug him, never listen to his laughter or his corny jokes.

Her throat tightened, her eyes burning with unshed tears.

When Jay said goodbye, she nodded and mumbled a response, but the words barely made it past her grief.

Marcus was silent as he pulled away from the house.

She expected him to stay that way.

What was the appropriate thing to say in the face of someone's grief? *I'm sorry* was never enough. No words could ease the ache of sorrow. Time dulled the pain but didn't erase it.

He touched her hand, his palm resting lightly over her knuckles. He was warm and solid, his presence oddly soothing. She had never imagined finding someone to spend her life with. She had imagined being released from prison. She had imagined finding her father's killer. She had imagined plenty of things, but having a relationship hadn't been one of them.

Kinsley had planned to spend her life alone.

She had thought it would be too difficult to share her story and her heart. She hadn't wanted to be vulnerable. She hadn't wanted to love. Those things meant the possibility of being hurt.

"I wish I could make this easier," Marcus said, the gentleness in his voice breaking her iron control.

A tear slid down her cheek.

She brushed it away impatiently.

"It's okay to cry."

"Maybe, but what good does it do?" she asked. "It can't bring my father back, and it can't bring his killer to justice."

"You're right. It can't, but maybe it can help your heart heal a little." He pulled into her driveway and parked behind the truck.

"I don't want to heal if it means I forget."

"Your father? You know that isn't going to happen."

"That he never got justice. That finding his killer is my responsibility."

"It isn't," he said, his voice sharp, his gaze sharper. "It is the responsibility of the police."

"Who have not been doing their job."

"They've been doing what they can. This is a cold case."

"Put on the back burner because it doesn't matter anymore. Not to law enforcement. Everyone who cared is either dead or retired."

"I care. And I'm neither of those things." He nearly growled the words, his eyes flashing with frustration.

"I'm talking about the police in Florida," she countered. "It's their case."

"You're talking about law enforcement in general. And I'm part of that."

"I know you're doing your best, Marcus. I

know you're trying, that you're digging, that you want to find answers, but in the end, when push comes to shove and it's all weighed out, he was my father. I have a responsibility to him."

"And *I* have a responsibility to you," he replied. "To my office, to my badge, and to the justice system I believe in."

Marcus got out of the vehicle.

She did the same.

"You're angry," she said as she fished keys out of her purse and led the way up to the apartment. She hadn't meant to upset him, and she felt unsettled and unsure.

"Angry? No. Concerned? Absolutely." He stepped into the apartment behind her and closed the door.

"You don't have to be. I know how to take care of myself."

"So did your father," he said quietly.

"He trusted the wrong person," she countered. "He was betrayed by someone close to him."

"That's what you think?"

"It's what I know."

"Then it is also someone you were close to. That's what concerns me," he said, his hands settling on her shoulders, his thumbs resting against the column of her neck.

She understood what he was saying.

She knew why he was concerned.

"I can't stop pursuing this. You know that, Marcus."

"Not even if I asked you to?"

He was staring into her eyes and she couldn't make herself look away. She wanted to tell him what he wanted to hear: that she would back off. That she would stop asking questions and making phone calls, that she would stop paying the private investigator.

She couldn't.

"Don't ask me," she responded, her heart in her throat.

"I'm working hard to get answers from Wright. I've put extra manpower into keeping you safe while we're waiting for that to happen."

"I appreciate that. I appreciate you." She touched his cheek, her palm resting on warm skin. He covered her hand with his.

"Good, because I don't think you're going to appreciate what I have to say."

"But you're going to say it anyway?" she asked wryly.

"I have a friend in Seattle who owns a security firm. He specializes in keeping high-powered clients safe. The company has several safe houses—"

"No," she said before he could finish, her hand dropping away from his cheek. "I'm not hiding in a safe house while you search for my father's killer."

"Because you'd rather be used as bait to draw him out."

It wasn't a question, but she nodded. "We've had this discussion before. You know my position on it."

"This isn't a boardroom. I'm not interested in your position on the issue. I'm interested in keeping you alive."

"It isn't like I want to die," she retorted.

"No?" He studied her face. "Then how about you start focusing on living. Instead of…" He stopped, pressing his lips together.

"Instead of what?"

"I don't want to tell you to let go of the past, Kinsley, but maybe it's time to start living in the moment and thinking about the future a little more."

"I am."

"You're not," Marcus corrected gently. "You're so caught up in your bid for justice, you've lost sight of one important fact. You have a life to live and a million new memories to build. If you spend all your time focused on where you came from, how can you appreciate where you are or figure out where you're going?"

His hand was on the doorknob, and she thought he was going to leave.

"I'm sorry," she murmured, wishing she could give him what he wanted. "I'd go into hiding but…" She didn't complete the thought.

How could she tell someone who had been fighting so hard for her that she didn't trust anyone but herself to find her father's killer? How could she even begin to explain the sick dread that filled her when she thought about walking away and letting law enforcement officials finish what she had begun?

"You don't trust anyone but yourself?" he asked, somehow reading her thoughts.

"No. I don't."

"Not even me?"

She was staring straight into his eyes, seeing the sadness and anger and defeat there.

"Marcus—"

"No answer is an answer, Kinsley," he said, taking a step closer and cupping her face in his hands. "Call me if you change your mind about the safe house." He kissed her tenderly, then walked out and down the stairs.

She could have stopped him.

She even wanted to.

But she didn't.

"Coward," she whispered as she closed the apartment door.

Her voice broke and she swallowed tears.

She wouldn't cry.

She *wouldn't*.

But, somehow, tears slid down her cheeks and dripped onto her shirt.

It wasn't his frustration or his anger that undid her.

It was his kindness.

His tenderness.

His understanding.

She had longed for those things for years and never had them. Now she had them and she was throwing them all away.

For what?

Justice for her father?

It was a righteous cause, but was it the right one?

How many times had Elizabeth told her to let God do His work? She had supported Kinsley's efforts, but she hadn't been enthusiastic about them. Doris had been the same. They both wanted the killer brought to justice, but not at the risk of Kinsley's happiness and well-being.

Or her life.

She paced the apartment, feeling hemmed in and trapped but afraid to step outside. She knew she was in danger. She couldn't deny that. She also couldn't deny her feelings for Marcus. The way she felt when he was around was unexpected but not unwelcome. Despite what she'd said—or hadn't said—she trusted him.

She knew she should call and tell him that, but she was afraid of what he might say. Afraid of rejection. Afraid of so many things that were outside of her control.

She made a cup of tea, left it to cool on the counter. Tried to focus on a book, then on the television. Her mind kept jumping from thought to thought. From the past to the present.

Her cell phone rang and she jumped.

She answered quickly, assuming it was Marcus.

Hoping it was him.

She needed to apologize. She needed to tell him that, of all the people she knew, he was the one she trusted most.

"I'm glad you called…" she began.

"And I'm glad I caught you. I thought you'd be working hard at the bakery today." Elizabeth's voice filled the line, the words clipped, the tone terse. Typical Elizabeth style of greeting.

"Elizabeth! How are you?"

"Cold. I'm not made for Montana winters."

"Montana?" Kinsley asked. "You're in Florida."

"Honey, did you really think I'd leave you to deal with your uncle alone after I was the one who told him how to contact you? I wouldn't. So, I took a day off work, and here I am. Outside, sitting in my rental, freezing to death."

"Outside?" Kinsley looked out the window.

A dark blue Corolla idled near her truck.

"You're really here?" she cried, unlocking the apartment door.

Before she could open it, the door flew inward, slamming into her and knocking her backward.

She fell, landing on the floor with enough force to bash the wind from her lungs.

A dark figure rushed at her, and she scrambled backward. Confused. Unsure. Just knowing she needed to get away. Get a weapon. Fight.

Kinsley was on her knees, on her feet, trying to run.

Something hit the back of her neck and she felt a quick zap and a moment of pain. Then she was on the floor, helpless, desperate to move and unable to.

A Taser. The thought flitted through her mind. Useless knowledge. Too late to do anything with.

The dark figure hunched above her, syringe in hand. She felt the quick sting of the needle, tried to fight the hands that pulled her up.

"Come on. Let's get you out of here before

any of your friends show up. We still have to collect Jay—and that might take some time."

Elizabeth?

Kinsley's thoughts were sluggish, her body leaden, as she was half carried, half dragged down the stairs. She tried to fight, but every movement was difficult, every thought slowed.

She was shoved into the back seat of the Corolla, her body sliding helplessly. Unable to do anything, Kinsley could only watch as the door closed.

She tried to stay conscious, to fight the drug she'd been given, but darkness edged in, the swish of tires on pavement the last thing she heard before everything faded away.

Marcus was in the middle of an all-out battle of wills when his cell phone rang. He set the book he'd been trying to get Rosie to read on the table.

"You need to finish the chapter before I'm off the phone, Rosemarlyn," he said.

"I told you, Uncle Marcus, I read this book last year." Rosemarlyn sighed dramatically. "What's the point of reading it again?"

"The point is your teacher assigned the reading. There are questions to answer—"

"That I could have answered last year when I read the book."

"That you are going to answer tonight," he corrected.

"But it's the weekend. I can—"

"Rosie, read the chapter. Answer the questions." The phone had stopped ringing. He glanced at the Caller ID, hoping to see Kinsley's number.

The fact that she didn't trust him stung more than he wanted it to, but he could understand her reasons. He had planned to tell her that. He'd called her twice, leaving messages both times. She hadn't returned his calls. He'd told himself that she was busy with her uncle, but he had worried it was something else. That she had decided to cut him out of her life and move forward without him.

He wanted to be okay with that.

He wasn't.

For a guy who had been certain he would spend his life as a bachelor, feeling concerned about the state of a relationship was novel. He didn't much like it.

But he did like Kinsley.

He was falling hard for her.

And he cared enough about their relationship to be disappointed when Charlotte's number flashed across the screen. She was on duty. Unless something big was happening, she wouldn't be calling him.

Concerned, he hit Redial.

"Marcus here, what's up?" he asked when she answered.

"Kinsley is missing."

"Missing?" His heart stopped then started again, flying forward at a frantic pace.

"I went by the house to grab something for lunch. When I pulled in next to her truck, I noticed the apartment door was open. She wasn't there. I tried to call her, but it went straight to voice mail."

"Did you call Doris?"

"She hasn't seen her since early this morning. You were the next person on my list to contact."

"We went to pick up her uncle at the airport. I dropped her off at her apartment after that."

"How long ago?" Charlotte asked.

"A little over an hour."

"Do you have contact information for her uncle?"

"No phone number, but we dropped him at Doris's."

"I'll call her place. If Jay doesn't pick up, I'll contact Doris again to see if she has his number."

"I'm heading to your place. Have you looked at the security footage?" he asked, grabbing his coat and calling a quick goodbye to Winnie and Rosie.

"I'm pulling it up. Now that I have a time-frame, I can narrow the footage down."

"I'll be there in ten."

He jumped in the SUV and sped into town, his heart beating wildly. He wanted to believe that nothing was wrong and that Kinsley had gone somewhere with Jay, but his gut told him this wasn't simply a case of someone being in one place when they were supposed to be in another.

Missing.

The word had a hollow ring to it.

Emptiness where there should be fullness.

Things went missing all the time. People went missing, too. Usually, it was nothing. A mistake. A miscommunication.

Sometimes it was something.

He pulled into Charlotte's driveway, jumping from the SUV and racing toward her house.

"I'm up here!" she called from the top of the apartment stairs. "I've called in every available officer. They should be responding soon."

She hadn't asked permission, and she didn't explain why.

He knew.

Without asking.

Without seeing the security footage.

He bounded up the stairs and would have

raced into the apartment if Charlotte hadn't raised a hand to stop him.

"Let's not contaminate evidence."

"Evidence of what?" he growled, adrenaline pulsing through him. He wanted action. He wanted results.

But first, he needed information.

"I believe she was abducted."

"You're not certain?"

"She opened the door willingly, and she left with help."

"What does that mean?"

She handed him her phone and pressed Play on a video she'd paused.

He watched as a blue car pulled up behind Charlotte's truck. Someone dressed in dark pants and a dark coat exited the vehicle and walked up the stairs. Whoever it was appeared to be on the phone. Seconds later, that person shoved open the apartment door and stepped inside, reemerging with Kinsley.

"Kinsley isn't struggling," Charlotte pointed out.

"She's not going willingly either," he replied, cold terror racing through him. "We need to get a read on the plate number and the make of the vehicle."

"I tried to read the plate number. It's obstructed. I think there's dirt on it, but I'm not certain. I do have the make and model of the car. Toyota Corolla."

"Dark blue."

"You issued a BOLO on the car?"

"Yes." Charlotte glanced down at the driveway as two marked cruisers pulled in. "Looks like backup is here. You want me to call in the state?"

"I want everyone and anyone who can help," Marcus replied, pushing aside his fear for Kinsley.

He had to focus and follow procedures. He had to think like the career officer he was. The straightest route out of town was down Main Street, but if the driver knew the area, there were plenty of ways to escape.

"Call Dispatch. Have them post a public appeal on Facebook. We want anyone who has seen that car to come forward. Also, anyone on your street who has a security camera."

"Already done."

"Call Doris's number. See if Jay picks up."

She did as he asked, then shook her head. "No answer."

"I'm going to Doris's place."

"You're not on duty."

"I am now." He jogged down the stairs, jumped into his SUV and headed to Doris's house.

It took minutes to get there. It felt like an eternity.

Every cell in his body was shouting for him to hurry.

The police officer in him was demanding he slow down, think things through, make rational decisions that would give them the best chance of finding the victim alive.

Victim.

He didn't want to think of Kinsley that way.

He didn't want to believe that it was already too late.

He prayed it wasn't.

Doris was standing on her front porch when he pulled up, an apron tied around her waist, a piece of paper in her hand.

She ran up to him, nearly tripping in her haste. "He's gone to meet Kinsley. He left a note. They're together."

She shoved the paper into his hand.

The note was brief. Just a few words.

Meeting Kinsley at the lake. Will be back to treat you to dinner. Jay.

"Did he take your car?" he asked.

"My car?" Doris frowned. "I didn't leave him

the keys. He said he didn't have a work meeting until tomorrow. Maybe Kinsley picked him up?"

"Her truck is at her place."

"They might have walked." She was grasping at straws.

He didn't tell her that.

She knew. He could see the fear in her eyes.

"Maybe he misunderstood where they were going?" he offered.

He didn't believe that.

He doubted she did.

"Or a friend of Kinsley's gave them a ride."

What friend? he wanted to ask.

They both knew that Kinsley hadn't made connections in Frenchtown. She had kept to herself, worked hard and avoided the kind of relationships that would have offered her a network of support.

He studied the note. *Meeting Kinsley at the lake.*

There were hundreds of lakes within driving distance.

If Kinsley had arranged a meeting, she would have given a specific name.

His cell phone rang. He answered quickly.

"Hello?"

"Marcus? It's Charlotte. Dispatch posted to Facebook and we already have leads. Jet Weber saw the vehicle heading out of town. Did you find anything there?"

"A note that says Jay is meeting Kinsley at the lake."

"Is that possible?" she asked.

"Not unless they walked."

"There aren't any lakes within walking distance," Charlotte pointed out.

"Exactly."

"Do you think Jay kidnapped her? I watched the news footage after her trial. He had an axe to grind with her. Could he have come to town for revenge?"

Maybe.

Or maybe someone else was pulling the strings and making things happen.

"Let's focus on getting her back. Then we'll focus on why this happened," he replied. "Which direction was the vehicle that Jet saw heading?"

"North. The closest lake in that direction is Old Man's Wish."

"Same place we were nearly shot, and probably familiar to whoever hired Wright." He didn't want to imagine Kinsley being brought to the lake and tossed into the icy water, but that's where his mind went. It's all he could see. All he could think about.

How long could someone survive in water that cold?

"You think that's where she is?" Charlotte asked.

"I hope it is. Meet me here. We'll head out together."

"How many other officers?"

"As many as can respond. No lights. No sirens. We don't want to scare the perp."

Scared people acted irrationally.

Kinsley was already in danger.

He didn't want to escalate things.

The results could be deadly.

Marcus winced away from the thought. There was still time to save Kinsley.

He wouldn't believe anything else.

TWELVE

She was cold.

Colder than she ever remembered being.

Floating.

Water lapping against the shore.

Camping?

No. She hadn't been since she was a child. She and her father and grandparents setting in a pop-up trailer at the edge of the Everglades. She almost drifted away on the memory of better times and warmer places, but something was wrong. Her tongue felt thick, her throat dry, her muscles heavy.

She forced her eyes open, wincing as bright sunlight seared them. She closed them again, ready to give in to the velvety cocoon of darkness. Something nudged her leg. A quick, light knock that brought her closer to the edge of wakefulness.

"You don't have to do this," a man said, the

words filtering through the soft lap of water and the hushed swish of blood in her ears.

"Of course I do," a woman replied.

Kinsley recognized both voices, but her mind was working sluggishly, making connections at a snail's pace. She kept her eyes closed, suddenly afraid and not sure why. Something had happened.

What?

She combed through her memories, but they were scattered like fallen leaves on a windy day. Skittering and flying each time she tried to examine them.

"Then maybe I should have said, you can't get away with it."

The woman laughed, the sound sending chills up Kinsley's spine.

"Of course, I can get away with this. I haven't been pegged for Michael's murder. I won't be pegged for this."

The words were like a splash of ice water in the face. Kinsley nearly jolted upright, but something held her still. That fear. That knowledge that something was very wrong.

"You convinced me it was Kinsley," the man growled.

Her father's voice, but not him.

Jay.

She'd picked him up at the airport. Dropped him off at Doris's house.

Why was he with her now?

Her mind was working again, the woman's comments like a shot of adrenaline straight into the heart.

Elizabeth!

She had orchestrated all of this.

"Someone had to be blamed and, you have to admit, she was a believable suspect. Spoiled little rich girl whose daddy gave her too much. I told Michael that she'd end up in trouble if he didn't keep a tighter rein on her. He insisted she was a good kid. That she'd find her way. And look what happened! She spent nearly twenty years in jail. All because he didn't listen."

"All because you killed him and framed Kinsley."

"I didn't kill anyone," Elizabeth snapped.

"Then you paid someone."

"Of course I did. I don't like getting my hands dirty. You've known me for how long? Twenty-five years? How could you not have known that?" The cold, condescending tone was as familiar as the rising sun or the crisp feel of winter air, but the words were foreign, the meaning so unbelievable, Kinsley almost jolted upright.

Elizabeth had had her father killed?

Why?

The question shouted through Kinsley's mind, demanding that she voice it.

She stayed silent, foggy memories returning.

Marcus. The way he'd looked when she'd told him she didn't trust anyone except herself. The quiet pad of his feet on the stairs as he'd left. Her phone ringing. Elizabeth's voice.

Elizabeth.

The closest thing to a mother she'd ever had.

One of just a few people who had stood in her corner and believed in her innocence was responsible for her father's murder.

"Why?" Jay asked, his voice anguished, the question one Kinsley was desperate to hear the answer to.

"I took some money to botch a federal case I was prosecuting. It was a lucrative deal and allowed me to invest in some real-estate ventures. Unfortunately, Michael wouldn't stop asking where I'd gotten the funds. He was a curious guy, remember?"

"You killed him," Jay said, obviously as shocked as Kinsley felt, "because you took a bribe?"

"Not just one. Several. I was smart about it, of course. I'd let junior members of the firm take the cases to trial. Always because *I trusted them and wanted to give them an opportunity to shine.*" She snickered. "It is easy to sabotage a case. If you know what you're doing. Harder not to get caught. You have to be smart, space things out, make certain the people who pay you don't talk. With enough money, silence is guaranteed. Of course, I made the mistake of getting involved with Michael. I thought he'd be a good front. Make me look respectable, altruistic."

"Altruistic? *You killed him.*"

"You've mentioned that. The fact is, though, I didn't kill him. I have someone who does that kind of work for me. And, honestly, if Michael had just left things alone, if he had just listened when I'd told him I had the money in savings, he would still be alive. We'd be married. Maybe we'd even have children. Instead, he started digging into my business. He began talking to interns at the law firm. He even talked to a few of the junior attorneys. I still don't know how he tracked them down. I didn't give him names and, once they lost the cases, they left the firm."

"You can't seriously be blaming my brother for what you did."

"Whose fault would it be, if it is wasn't his?"

"Yours."

"Please. Taking money to throw white-collar cases? What's criminal about that? Our justice system is overburdened anyway. I was doing the prison system a favor."

"You were breaking the law. You had to know my brother wouldn't approve."

"I thought your brother was malleable. I thought he would take what I said at face value and leave things alone. If he had... Well, we've already covered that, haven't we? Are you trying to buy time, Jay?"

"I'm trying to understand why my brother had to die." His voice broke.

"You're soft. Just like him. If you weren't, you would understand."

"Did he know it was you?" he asked, the heartbreak in his voice matching the ache in Kinsley's heart.

"I didn't pull the trigger, but he knew the man who did. Andrew Wright was my personal assistant for a while. I paid him under the table, so there was no record, but Michael met him once or twice." She sounded disinterested and unaffected. "I paid Andrew to disappear a year before the murder. He'd already done a few jobs for me. He liked the money as much as I did."

"You could have disappeared, too. Instead of killing Michael."

"Not if I were going to achieve my political aspirations. Which I was."

"You can still disappear," he said. "Just let me paddle us back to shore, and you can get in the car and go wherever you want."

"You're pretty demanding. For a man who has a gun pointed at his heart."

A gun?

Kinsley's pulse bounded, sending adrenaline pumping through her and pushing aside the last bit of lethargy and confusion.

"I should have refused to come outside when you called me. I thought it was strange that you were in town."

"Strange. Yes. I guess it was." Elizabeth laughed, the sound sending a chill up Kinsley's spine. "I'm sure it seemed even stranger that I had a gun."

"If you're going to shoot me, go ahead. I won't be part of whatever you have planned for Kinsley."

"Die and leave your wife and precious kids? I don't think you want to do that, Jay. Especially not now that you know what I'm capable of." Elizabeth's voice was cold as an Arctic wind.

Jay didn't respond and, for a moment, Kinsley could hear nothing but the soft lap of water against...what?

A boat hull?

She focused on the sound and on the cold that had seeped into her bones. Not just cold. She was wet, lying in a puddle.

Something nudged her leg again.

Not as gently as the first time. Harder and more insistent.

Kinsley cracked open her eyes, tried to look around without moving her head. She saw a pant leg and the metal side of what had to be a boat. No motor running, but she was certain they were on a lake. She wiggled her toes, her fingers, made certain she had feeling in her limbs. She'd been taken by surprised and knocked unconscious, but that didn't mean the fight was over.

She could almost hear Marcus's safety talks, the ones she had heard every time she'd attended his self-defense classes.

It isn't over until you're no longer breathing. Fight with the idea that you will *win.*

She shifted slightly, trying to figure out where she was and where Elizabeth was.

Her friend.

Her father's former fiancée.

A woman who had hired a hitman to make sure her secrets stayed hidden.

Kinsley couldn't wrap her mind around that.

She couldn't quite make herself believe that Elizabeth was responsible for her father's death.

"I see you've decided not to leave your wife and kids to my disposal," Elizabeth said, her voice echoing loudly in the quiet. There were no birds singing. No whispers of leaves as the breeze wafted through. Just that soft drip and lap of water.

"No one wants to die," Jay said, and Kinsley felt something hit her foot. A kick maybe. Not hard, but enough to make her leg move.

Was Jay trying to get her attention?

Wake her up?

Warn her?

"But I know you plan on killing me whether I cooperate or not, so I'm not sure why you're bothering to threaten my wife and my kids." Jay sounded calm and reasonable.

If he was afraid, he was hiding it.

"Here's the deal, Jay. I'm not a monster. I'm not evil. I'm just a woman with goals. If you help me accomplish them, I'll have no reason to bother your wife or your children. If you don't, I will make their lives miserable."

"You don't have that kind of power."

"You keep forgetting the money part of the equation. Why do you think I wanted it? Why did I take those bribes? Why did I invest in real estate and marry a millionaire twenty years my senior? People with money have power. Now, here is what is going to happen. You're going to dump Kinsley out of the boat, then you are going to row us back to shore. Not where I parked. The opposite side of the lake."

"I'm not hurting my niece," Jay growled.

"That's fine. Choose her over your wife, your children. Maybe that is the nobler path. After all, you did throw her to the wolves when she was arrested. How many stories about her rebellion did you tell the police? And, how many times did you say you thought she might be capable of killing Michael?"

"You convinced me of that. You planted the idea in my head. I never would have believed it otherwise."

"Convinced you? You wanted to believe it. You wanted there to be a reason Michael was murdered. Kinsley's rebellion was as good a one as any for your brother's death. So, you listened to every word I told you, and then you repeated it. You did what I wanted, and I didn't even have to pay you." She chuckled gleefully. "Power isn't all about money, after all. It's also about knowing how to get people to do your bidding."

"You are an evil person, Elizabeth. I can't believe I didn't see it until now," he seethed.

"Evil? Please. I'm just a woman who knows what she wants. I'm willing to do what is necessary to get it. Now, make your choice quickly. Toss her in. Or I'll do it and then deal with your wife and your kids."

"And me?" he asked grimly. "You certainly aren't going to let me go."

"You know what most people don't understand, Jay?"

"I'm sure you're going to tell me."

He kicked Kinsley's ankle.

"What are you doing? Trying to wake her before you toss her!" Elizabeth nearly shrieked.

The boat bobbed and tilted.

Water sloshed in.

"I was trying to figure out the best way to pick her up," he replied.

He was lying. Kinsley knew it.

Elizabeth had to know it.

Jay was running out of time, and he was trying to buy more. If he bought enough, would help come? Did anyone know Kinsley was missing? She'd created a habit of distancing herself from the people around her. She rubbed shoulders with plenty of bakery patrons and fellow church members, but she didn't have deep friendships that garnered daily communication.

"The best way to do it is to do it," Elizabeth attested.

The boat tilted, water slopping in and pooling near Kinsley's head.

"Get it done, Jay. You won't like what happens if you don't."

"Did you ever love my brother?" he hedged.

Kinsley could feel his tension, sense the way his muscles had tightened.

He was getting ready for something.

To toss her into the lake?

She could swim, but the water was frigid. She'd be hypothermic in minutes.

"What does love have to do with anything? I *liked* Michael. He treated me well. If he hadn't been digging into my personal business, he'd still be alive and we wouldn't all be sitting out in the cold. I'm not made for this weather. Let's get this done!" she barked.

"Love has everything to do with everything I have ever done," Jay said quietly, the grief in his voice making Kinsley's heart ache. He had a family waiting for him. A wife he loved. Children. He had to be thinking about them, wondering if he would ever see them again.

"I said, let's get it done. Now!" Elizabeth yelled.

Kinsley opened her eyes. She wanted to see what was coming, so she could fight it.

But Jay didn't reach for her. Instead, he lunged across her.

The sharp report of a bullet nearly deafened Kinsley.

She sat up, watching in horror as Jay toppled over the side of the boat.

Blood seeped into the water, dark purple in the azure lake.

"This wasn't how I wanted it to happen, but

so be it," Elizabeth muttered. She was sitting in the bow, dressed in black jeans and black jacket, the hood pulled over her hair, her face nearly hidden by it. She held a gun in her gloved hand, the barrel pointing down.

"What did you do?" Kinsley asked, reaching over the side of the boat, grabbing the back of Jay's jacket. Frantic. Praying.

Please, God, don't let him be dead.

"I took care of a problem, Kinsley. Now, I guess I have to take care of you."

Elizabeth raised the gun, aiming it at Kinsley's head, her face contorted in a mixture of rage and hatred. "I never did like you, you know. You were just something I had to put up with to be with Michael."

Fight until you can't. Marcus's words filled her head and Kinsley grabbed Elizabeth's gun arm, wrenching it up. A shot rang out, the bullet flying wild.

The boat tilted.

The world tilted.

She fell into Elizabeth, her fingers locking around her wrist. Fighting for control. Fighting for the chance to save her uncle. She slammed Elizabeth's hand into the side of the boat. Once. Twice.

The gun fell into the water.

"You're going to pay for that!" Elizabeth bellowed, shoving her backward.

Kinsley tumbled over the side of the boat.

Icy water filled her nose and lungs.

She bobbed to the surface, gasping.

Jay! She had to get him to safety.

The cold water made her movements sluggish. She blinked to clear her eyes, turning in a circle until she spotted Jay. He was a few feet away, the boat beside him.

She grabbed the back of his jacket, hauling him over so that his face was out of the water. His lips were blue. She tried to feel for a pulse, but her fingers were too cold.

"Jay?" she shouted in his ear as she tugged him farther away from the boat. The shore was a distant landscape of rocks and greenery. She kicked in that direction. She was already too cold. Already panting hard.

"You're not going to win this, Kinsley. You were never going to win. From the very beginning, you were an unimportant player who had a very minor role. The red herring. The easy way to keep the authorities from looking at me," Elizabeth called dispassionately.

She was sitting.

Watching.

Waiting for Kinsley to die?

Kinsley couldn't think about that.

She couldn't allow herself time for anger or fear.

She had to focus on saving herself and her uncle.

The dark blue Toyota was parked near an old dock.

Marcus saw it as they reached the end of the access road.

"That has to be the car we saw in the security footage," Charlotte muttered. "It looks abandoned."

"I'll check it out."

He jumped from the cruiser and ran to the abandoned vehicle. The doors were closed but unlocked. He used gloved hands to pop the trunk.

No bags.

No blood.

No body.

Thank you, Lord. The prayer whispered through his mind as he scanned the small beach area and the water.

"There was a boat tied to the dock the last time I was here," Charlotte said as she reached his side.

"When was that?"

"When we investigated the shooting."

"I was too preoccupied to notice."

"It's gone now. We need to search the lake," Charlotte responded.

"We'll need a boat. Remember Ken Milton?"

"Police officer who retired last year? How could I forget? He helped train me."

"He lives a mile from here. And he has a fishing boat."

"I'll call to see if he can bring it." She grabbed her cell phone and started dialing.

Several police cruisers were pulling in behind Charlotte's vehicle. A state K-9 unit followed, the SUV edging around the other vehicles and parking close to the water.

Plenty of manpower for a search.

They just had to organize and deploy.

That took time.

Time Kinsley didn't have.

Marcus shoved down the hard knot of worry, pushed aside everything except the goal. Find Kinsley. Bring her home safely. He ran onto the dock, stopping at the end of it, the soft rotting wood giving slightly beneath his feet.

"Ken is on the way," Charlotte said as she joined him. "The lake is huge, Marcus. If she's in it—"

"We'll find her," he said, his attention caught by a speck on the surface of the lake. "You see that?" he asked, pointing toward it.

"Yeah. Is it a boat?"

"There's only one way to find out. Get out there."

"I'll see if Ken is on the road." She ran.

He waited. Watched the speck.

Was it moving closer?

Getting farther away?

Marcus felt helpless; unable to do anything but wait for Ken's boat to arrive, but desperate to do something. Dark clouds covered the sun, the watery light reflecting off the lake. A slight breeze rippled across the water's surface. It was a beautiful day to be on the lake. Not a good one to be in it. Runoff from the melting mountain snow fed the rivers, creeks and streams, keeping lake waters cold for most of Montana's springs.

A person could survive for a limited amount of time in frigid water. An injured person had even less time.

"Don't think about it," he chided aloud. "Focus on the plan."

"He's here!" Charlotte yelled. "Bringing the boat up to the water."

Marcus watched as Ken Milton sped into view, a trailer hitched to the back of his pickup hauling a small fishing vessel with a motor on the back.

Marcus hurried to help him unload, guiding the boat into knee-deep water, the cold seeping into his bones.

If Kinsley was in the water, she had very little time.

"This thing'll fit four or five people. In a pinch," Ken said, his green eyes hidden behind dark sunglasses. "The motor can be finicky, so you either need to let me come along, or you need to be prepared to stall out a few times."

"We don't have time to stall," Marcus responded, holding the boat and gesturing for Ken to get in.

The speck was still out there.

Maybe a little larger.

Moving toward them for sure.

Or, at least, not moving away.

"Chief," Charlotte said, "do you want me to come with you?"

"No." Marcus settled into the bow of the boat, the gun holster Charlotte had brought him from the office banging against his thigh. His radio was in a chest pack, the antenna banging his cheek. He hadn't asked Charlotte to stop for either. She'd done it because she'd known both might be necessary.

She'd sacrificed minutes on the chance it might save lives.

She was a good officer.

Clear-headed and quick. Charlotte made good decisions about tough things, and he probably would have been smart to let her take his place in the boat.

Emotion clouded things.

It made action more complicated.

But Kinsley was in trouble, and he needed to find her. To help her. To bring her home.

"See if you can get a state water rescue team out. We might need divers," he said, his voice gritty with fear.

He didn't want to think that divers would be necessary.

He didn't want to imagine never finding Kinsley.

In lakes like this one, that happened.

People were dragged in by undercurrents and never seen again.

"Not this time," he whispered.

"Where are we heading?" Ken asked.

"I thought I saw something toward the middle of the lake. There." Marcus pointed. The thing he had seen was clearer now, bobbing on the surface and glinting in the cloud-muted sunlight.

"Looks like a boat," Ken commented.

"It does."

"If there's a boat, there are people. You think they're armed?"

"I don't know. If you want to abort the mission, I can bring Charlotte with me."

"Nah. I miss work. Sitting around in my recliner isn't as interesting as I thought it would be. I'll take you out there, but I'm glad I wore a Kevlar vest." Ken yanked the pull cord on the motor. It sputtered. He pulled again and it caught, the sound chasing birds from nearby trees.

They would have had to shout to speak over it.

Marcus didn't plan to waste the energy.

His focus was on the thing bobbing in the water.

First just a glint on the surface, then, as they approached, taking shape. A metal canoe. Green hull. Old. Someone sitting in it, an old wooden oar in hand, looking at something in the water.

A person? People?

Red hair floating on the lake.

Dark blood in the water.

Kinsley.

Jay.

She had her arm around her uncle's chest, pulling him away from the canoe, sluggishly moving through the water, her face pale, her teeth visibly chattering.

Marcus's pulse jumped, his heart slamming against his ribs.

"Stop the motor!" he shouted, afraid the wake would overwhelm her.

Ken cut the motor.

The world went silent except for the soft slap of water against metal.

The person in the canoe didn't move. Simply watched their approach, face hidden by the hood of the jacket.

"You two need to leave." The woman's voice seemed to bounce across the surface of the water. Hollow, but demanding.

Marcus studied what he could see of her face and realized that he knew exactly who she was.

"Elizabeth Harvey?" he called back.

"For today, by tomorrow, I'll be someone else. I'm sorry you won't be informed of my new name." She laughed, shifting the oar into her lap and reaching beneath her jacket to pull out a firearm.

"Put it down," Marcus ordered, his focus on her hand, on the gun. His mind on Kinsley. On getting her and her uncle out of the water alive.

"I don't think so. You have two people to save. If you can. I have a new life to begin. So, you go to work. I'll just make my way out of here."

Did she really think it would be that easy?

"Stay where you are, ma'am, and put the weapon down," Marcus demanded as Ken reached for oars to maneuver their boat closer.

"Who's going to make me?" Elizabeth asked.

She seemed to be reveling in the moment, enjoying what she had caused. "You?" she mocked. "You're too busy trying to save people who are past saving. Kinsley is dying, Chief Bayne. And you're just sitting in the boat, letting it happen."

She knew who he was. That didn't surprise him.

A woman who had gotten away with murder, hadn't done so by being stupid.

They'd reached Kinsley, the boat just inches from her. His focus shifted.

"Elizabeth, do what he says," Kinsley pleaded, her voice weak. She was trying to keep her head above water, her uncle held against her chest as she'd tried to backstroke toward shore.

"Shut up, Kinsley," Elizabeth responded, her face contorted with rage, hatred. "My life was perfect. They were bandying my name around as a vice presidential candidate. A few more years and I'd have had exactly what I'd wanted. If you had just been happy to be free of prison. If you had just let that be enough. Instead, you had to poke and prod and ask questions and demand answers. You got the police riled up. I had to stop you. And if Andrew hadn't messed things up, I would have."

"My father—" Kinsley gasped "—deserves justice. He's going to get it."

"No, but he will get a meeting with you.

Sooner rather than later. You two can be re-united. Hopefully, Jay can be there, too. All of you having a family reunion in Heaven." Elizabeth raised the gun, pointed it. "I didn't want to do this. Not really, but you've pushed me to it. You've stolen everything I worked for. Everything. I'll have to recreate myself somewhere where no one knows me. Fortunately, I always plan an escape. Goodbye, Kinsley. I won't miss you. See you around, Chief Bayne."

"Put the weapon down," he commanded, his firearm out, his finger on the trigger before the loud report.

Too late.

She'd pulled the trigger, the bullet flying just as he'd aimed and fired a shot.

Elizabeth went down, came up again.

Reached for the oars, paddling hard.

He had hit her. Hadn't he?

He didn't know. Couldn't care.

Kinsley had disappeared beneath the surface of the water.

No sign of her or Jay.

He grabbed his radio, yelling for backup and for the dive teams. He couldn't lose Kinsley. Not when it had taken so long to find her. His life had been filled with people, with work, with Rosie and Winnie. Until Kinsley stepped into it, he hadn't realized how big a hole there'd been in his heart. He hadn't had any desire to fill the empty space with romantic love or dinner dates. He had felt content to be a bachelor, raising a child with the help of his aunt.

Now, he wanted more.

He wanted quiet dinners and loud family gatherings. He wanted walks in the moonlight, holding hands.

He wanted to grow with Kinsley, find their groove. He wanted to be there for her in every way that mattered. He wanted to show her that love could last, that friendships could be loyal and true.

"Kinsley?" he shouted, stripping off his coat.

He couldn't let her die.

He wouldn't.

She'd come too far, fought too hard for the freedom to live her life. He wouldn't see it end in the cold waters of the lake. Not if he could do anything to prevent it.

"Please, Lord. Help me save her," he prayed as he dove into the water and tried desperately to see into its murky depths.

He had to find her, help her, save her.

And, then, he had to tell her what he had known for weeks and tried to ignore.

He hadn't been looking for love.

He hadn't wanted to find it.

But he had.

He couldn't deny that.

He couldn't deny her or the way he felt when they were together. He loved Kinsley. As he struggled to find her in the darkness of the water, he could only pray he would have an opportunity to tell her.

THIRTEEN

She would die if she couldn't find the strength to resurface.

Jay would die.

Please God, she managed to pray as she pushed toward the surface, her lungs burning, her head pounding.

Just one more time up to the surface.

Marcus was there.

A boat was waiting.

She just had to make it to the light.

Kinsley focused on that—the gleaming edge of water that soaked in the light and filtered it toward her.

She'd ducked under because she had known Elizabeth would shoot. The woman had no heart, no conscious. She certainly would have no remorse. Shooting Kinsley would give her an opportunity to escape and, from what Kinsley had heard, it seemed opportunities were all Elizabeth cared about.

Did you ever love my brother? Jay had asked.

Elizabeth hadn't loved anyone.

She didn't seem to love anyone.

Not even her family.

Kinsley made it to the surface.

She gasped, her lungs shrinking as icy air filled them. She wanted out of the lake with more desperation than she had wanted out of prison. She would die if she didn't make it into the boat. Jay would die.

She kept her arm hooked under his and wrapped tightly around his chest. She thought he was breathing, thought she might have heard him groan.

"Kinsley!" Marcus shouted.

She tried to respond, but coughed instead, gagging on cold water, nearly sinking again.

She was going under.

She knew it.

And once she did, it would all be over. The fight would end, because she would have nothing more to fight with. Elizabeth would win.

"It's okay, I've got you." Marcus's arm wrapped around her shoulders. "Come on. We're almost out of here."

"We have to get Jay in the boat. He's been shot," she said, her teeth chattering so loudly, she wasn't sure he could understand the words.

"We have to get you both in the boat," he responded.

But he was cold, too. He had to be. His body pressed so close to hers, his muscles taut in response to the icy water, she could feel him trembling. Or maybe that was her, shaking with cold, trembling uncontrollably.

"Get him into the boat. I'll be fine until you do," she lied.

"I'm not letting go of you," he replied, paddling with one arm, dragging them up next to the boat.

"I've got a life buoy," a man called.

Something landed in the water beside them.

Kinsley reached for it with her free arm, her movements so uncoordinated, she pushed it away instead of pulling it close.

"Come on now, hon. You can do better than that," the man called. "I'm keeping my boat nice and steady. We're going to pull you in and take you home and warm you up, but first let's get your friend in. Grab that buoy and hold on, so Marcus can help me help you."

"Right," she muttered, reaching for it again, trying to make her frozen fingers do their part. She managed to hook it with her arm and pull it close, but she didn't want to release her hold on Jay. If he went under, they might never find him.

"You have to let him go so I can lift him," Marcus said as he grabbed the side of the boat.

"I can't. What if he slips in?" she replied, looking into Marcus's eyes, memorizing the deep chocolate and rich gold, the light green and gray. Hazel eyes filled with concern.

She loved him.

Kinsley realized it with a quiet start that filled her with wonder and with worry. She hadn't meant to love anyone.

"I won't let that happen," he said.

She hesitated, her body numb, the tremors ceasing. She was far into hypothermia now, and if she didn't get out of the water, she would die.

The rational part of her knew that.

The irrational part wanted to maintain control.

"Please, Kinsley, don't fight me on this," Marcus begged, and her heart shattered into pieces, all the hard places suddenly soft with longing for him.

"Marcus," she said as she released her hold on Jay, allowing Marcus to pull him toward the boat. "I need you to know something."

"Tell me when we're on shore," he replied, his focus on the man in the boat and on Jay, on maneuvering a deadweight into a floating vessel. He didn't have time to listen, and now wasn't the time to say it, but she was losing her grip on the world. Darkness was right at the edges of her mind. Taunting her and tempting her to just give up and let go.

"Now is better," she said as he managed to heft Jay up.

The boat swayed, the man in it pulled at Jay's shirt collar, gasping and muttering as he struggled to drag the soaked body onboard.

"I love you, Marcus. Don't forget it," she uttered, her grip on the buoy slipping.

She wanted to keep fighting for Doris, for Marcus and his family, for the future that suddenly seemed so pure and free of the past. She knew who her father's killer was. She knew why he had died. She could move on. But the water suddenly felt warm, the soft rhythm of the waves lulling her.

She thought someone said her name, but she was drifting on rays of Florida sunshine, remembering those long-ago camping trips and the starlit night sky. The Milky Way spreading across the horizon.

Her father laughing.

"Hold on, Kinsley," he said. "We're almost there."

Her arms tightened around him, but it was just the wet edge of the buoy, and someone whispering in her ear, "I love you, too."

* * *

The state dive team arrived just as Marcus lifted Kinsley up and into the boat. He could clearly hear their motorboat's engine.

Good.

He could use all the help he could get. His teeth were chattering, his muscles cramping from cold.

Kinsley was limp and lifeless. No more tremors. No teeth chattering. She was hypothermic, her body cold to the touch.

"Kinsley?" he shouted her name as Ken helped him get her into the boat. She landed in the stern. Unresponsive. Unconscious.

"You're next," Ken said, reaching for Marcus's arm and dragging him up and in. "I used my cell to call for an ambulance. This guy is pretty far gone, but he's still breathing," he said, shrugging out of his jacket and folding it into a bandage that he pressed against a bleeding wound in Jay's chest.

"Does he have a pulse?" Marcus asked, lifting Kinsley's wrist and probing the pulse point.

"Faint. Steady. It's possible she didn't hit anything vital, and the cold water may have protected him from organ damage. The sooner we get him to a hospital, the better. I told the 9-1-1 dispatcher we might need Life Flight. There's a clear area next to the road where they can land. We just need to get him there. How's she doing?"

Marcus could feel her pulse beating sluggishly. "She needs to get the hospital."

"No, she doesn't," Kinsley murmured, her lips blue, her eyes closed.

"I suppose you have a better idea?" He grabbed his coat, tucking it around her. The wind had picked up, storm clouds drifting across the sky.

Elizabeth was still paddling toward the distant shore. He watched as the boat veered in one direction and then another. She couldn't outrun the state police boats. She'd be caught, and she'd be jailed. Justice would be served, but the damage she'd done would remain.

"Yeah. Soft blankets. Roaring fire. Hot chocolate. The two of us and Rosie, watching her favorite cartoon," Kinsley replied, opening her eyes and struggling to sit.

He wrapped an arm around her waist and helped her onto the metal seat. "That's a phenomenal idea, Kinsley. After the doctor says you're okay."

"I'm fine." Her gaze shifted to Jay.

"He needs help. Jay?" She touched his hand.

"We've got Life Flight coming," Marcus assured her.

"Let's get back to shore so we can meet

them," Ken added, pulling the cord and starting the motor.

They passed the dive team as they headed for shore. Three uniformed officers sat in the motorboat. Two state officers and Charlotte. They waved but didn't stop, the vessel heading straight toward Elizabeth.

"I need to warn them that she's armed," he shouted above the engine noise, trying his radio, but not surprised when it didn't work.

"First, she fired a shot. I'm sure Charlotte heard it. Second, I called Charlotte on my cell while you were in the water. She's aware. They're going to get her before she reaches shore and hurts anyone else." Ken shook his head, his gaze focused on the dock and the emergency crew that had assembled there.

It took minutes to reach them. Just a little longer for the crew to stabilize Jay and lift him out of the boat. He remained unconscious, his skin mottled, blood staining his shirt.

"If he dies, it'll be my fault," Kinsley said quietly as a paramedic wrapped her in a blanket.

"No, it won't," Marcus replied, accepting the blanket he was offered and then drawing Kinsley in for a hug. She leaned her head against his chest, her hair falling across his knuckles as he rubbed her back.

"I really do love you," she whispered, the

words as surprising the second time as they had been the first.

Love was a big thing.

It was commitment.

It was friendship.

It was being part of someone's life without holding anything back.

But he wasn't afraid of those things. Kinsley fit his life the way no other woman ever had. She was kind, compassionate, hardworking and empathetic. She liked Rosie, got along well with Winnie, enjoyed small-town life. Her faith had carried her through more trials than most people would ever see, and he admired that.

And, when she had said she loved him, the last piece of a puzzle he hadn't realized he was working on had fallen into place.

"I thought you were delirious from cold when you said that the first time," he replied, leaning back to look into her face.

She was pale, her lips still purple, her body trembling as she began to warm up.

"I wasn't. I was just…"

"What?"

"Very aware that I might not survive. If I died, I wanted you to know how I felt."

"Did you hear my response?" he asked, brushing bangs from her eyes, his fingers lingering. Her skin was cold, but her cheeks were pink, her blush making him smile.

"I thought I did, but maybe you should repeat it. Just in case I misheard?"

"I said I love you." He kissed her gently then stepped away, his hand on her waist. "And we'll have that fire and cartoon-watching date, but first, I want you to get checked out the hospital."

"I need to go with Jay."

"There won't be room on the Life Flight chopper, but we can transport you," Marcus said. "I'll drive you. I'm not letting you out of my sight until Elizabeth is apprehended," Marcus commented, turning his attention to the lake.

The boat was returning.

It looked like Elizabeth was in it.

"I think they have her," he said.

"Thank the Lord," Kinsley replied.

"You two okay?" a state police officer asked as he approached.

"Fine," Marcus replied. "You've got Elizabeth Harvey in custody?"

"Yes. From what I heard on the radio, she didn't even put up a fight. Apparently, she has a gunshot wound to the right arm, and she's demanding immediate medical treatment."

"Not at the hospital where Jay is going to be!" Kinsley cried. "She's dangerous!"

"We're taking her to Sacred Heart," the police officer responded. "Don't worry. She's not going to escape. And she's not going to hurt anyone ever again."

"So, that's it?" Kinsley asked as he walked away.

It wasn't.

Marcus was certain she knew that.

There would be a trial. Elizabeth would be savvy enough to stretch the process out as long as possible. Eventually, though, justice would be served. She'd be in prison where she belonged, and Kinsley could go on with her life.

With *their* lives.

He liked the way that sounded, and the way she felt, tucked beneath his arm as he helped her into the ambulance.

The soft thump of helicopter rotors filled the air, mixing with the engine hum of the returning boat. Jay was being carried to the main road, the Life Flight crew and stretcher disappearing from view as the motorboat reached shore.

Elizabeth was helped off, her gaze darting around the shoreline. She was probably looking for an escape route. But there were dozens of officers around now, none of them impressed when she began shouting that she wanted a lawyer.

"She still thinks she can get out of this," Kinsley said quietly, her eyes filled with tears. "I can't believe she had my father murdered."

"I can't believe she was never a suspect," Marcus replied. He should have dug more deeply into her background. That was the direction the case had seemed to lead, but Andrew Wright's silence had meant no evidence that she was involved. Without just cause, no search warrants could be obtained.

Elizabeth had been smart.

She had made herself Kinsley's staunchest ally.

In doing so, she had turned attention away from herself.

"She was working behind the scenes, telling people stories about me and my supposed rebellion. She convinced me that she was helping, but really, she was turning everyone I knew against me."

"Including Jay?"

"Yes." A tear slipped down her cheek and she wiped it away impatiently. "I can't blame him for believing her. From what he said when we were on the boat, she'd been setting things up for a while."

"Why?" he asked.

"She was taking bribes to throw cases. Or, sabotage them. She used the money to fund real-estate ventures to help support her political campaigns."

"And your father found out?"

"Found out or was getting close. Andrew Wright was the shooter. She mentioned him. I would make sure he is separated from other inmates. I wouldn't put it past her to try to take him out to keep him from talking." She sighed, stepping back from the ambulance door and turning away from Elizabeth.

"We'll keep him safe, and maybe now that she has been arrested, he'll be willing to talk. An explanation of how she paid him without leaving an electronic trail would be nice, but it won't be necessary for a conviction. Not now."

"She's smart. She'll try to get out of it by blaming someone else," Kinsley said, dropping down onto the gurney as the EMT closed the doors.

"She can blame whomever she likes, but we have witnesses who heard her confess."

"I hope Jay is okay," she responded. "We have so much lost time to make up for."

"He will be." Marcus sat beside her and pulled her close. "And you will be, too. Eventually."

"How can I not be? I have you and Doris and Rosie and Winnie. A job I love in a town I love. All the old wounds will heal, and I'll build wonderful memories that will eventually over-shadow the difficult ones."

"You've already been building memories, Kinsley, and I'm glad I've been a part of them."

"I've been thinking," she said, her head still on his shoulder as the ambulance rolled away from the lake.

"About?"

"Doris will sell the bakery eventually. I'd like to buy it."

"Buy it?"

"Why not? I love working there. I'm good at it. It's an iconic part of town, and someone who loves it should maintain it. Don't you think?"

He did think that.

Just like he thought someone who loved her should nourish Kinsley's heart, give her all the things she hadn't had when she'd been locked away in prison—support, friendship, companionship.

"I do." He kissed her gently, sweetly, tasting salty tears on her lips. "You're crying." He pulled back, wiped the tears from her cheeks.

"It hurts—what Elizabeth did. But what God did? Bringing me here? Putting us into each other's lives? That's why I'm crying. It's beautiful, and lovely, and everything I never dreamed I could have."

"You have it. You have me," Marcus assured

her, kissing her again as the ambulance turned onto the main road and headed for the hospital.

He meant it.

No matter what the future brought. No matter the challenges they might face, he planned to stand beside Kinsley, supporting her the way she deserved. Just as he knew she would support him.

That was love.

Not something that happened for a moment.

Something that lasted a lifetime.

Kinsley reached for his hand, her fingers curving through his, and for the first time in more years than he could remember, the world felt completely right.

EPILOGUE

She made her own wedding cake.

What bride who could, wouldn't?

Kinsley placed the last flower on the top tier and stepped away from the display table. The church meeting hall had been decorated with flowers and candles, light dancing across the tables and spilling out from the inset windows.

Cream and white with hints of royal blue.

Nothing fancy.

She and Marcus hadn't wanted that.

They had wanted cozy and intimate. But the entire congregation of the church planned to attend the ceremony.

Which was—she glanced at her watch—ten minutes away!

She smoothed the 1950's dress her grandmother had once worn. After Kinsley's grandmother had died, Doris had kept it. A family heirloom she'd been hoping would one day be worn again. Today was the day. For that and for so many things.

Marcus had proposed six months after Elizabeth's arrest. Neither of them had wanted a protracted engagement. They knew what they had was real, that it would weather all the toughest storms. Doris, Winnie and Rosie had been ecstatic when they'd heard the news.

Just days after the proposal, Elizabeth had been tried and convicted of murder, plus two counts of attempted murder. Andrew Wright had done exactly what Marcus had suspected he would do. As soon as he'd heard that Elizabeth was in jail, he'd started to talk. He'd been paid in cash from a secret bank account Elizabeth had set up in Michael's name. Not something the police had ever bothered to look into, given the account had been opened in the months prior to his death. Even then, Elizabeth had been planning his murder.

Knowing that hurt, but the hurt of the past had begun to pale in comparison to the joy of the present.

"You're beautiful," Jay said, stepping into the room. "Michael would be so proud." His voice broke, and he dashed a tear away. He'd had a long and difficult road to recovery. Eight months after the shooting, he was finally doing well.

"I wish he could be here," Kinsley replied.

"If God gives glimpses of our loved ones while we're in Heaven, this will be the day that Michael sees you. I'm sure of it." He took her arm. "I don't want to rush you, but Marcus is at the front of the church, looking very handsome. His dog, Fitz, doesn't seem phased by the hubbub, but Rosie is tossing pedals all over the aisle runner, and Doris is starting to get antsy."

"So, it's time?" she asked, her heart leaping with nervous anticipation and joy.

"Yes. Are you ready?"

"I am." She took his arm, walking into the hall that led to the sanctuary.

Organ music swelled, drifting out into the corridor. Her heart swelled with it.

Kinsley had never expected to find a love like the kind she had with Marcus. Accepting and encouraging, he filled her life with laughter and adventure.

She couldn't imagine living a day without him.

She couldn't imagine what her life would have been like if they hadn't met.

She didn't want to imagine it.

Doris was waiting near the double doors, her royal-blue dress and bouquet of winter flowers making her look decades younger than she was. She had been cooking for days, prepping food for the in-church reception. She didn't look tired. She looked exuberant, her eyes sparkling with joy.

Winnie was beside her, her dress clinging to her curves, her hair falling to her shoulders.

She was holding Kinsley's bouquet, a soft smile on her face. "You are gorgeous," she said, pressing the bouquet into Kinsley's hands and grabbing her flowers from a chair nearby.

"My nephew is a very blessed man."

"I am a very blessed woman."

"None of us is going to feel blessed if Rosie tears the place apart while we're out here chatting in the hall," Doris said, sniffing back tears and smiling. "Your grandparents would be over the moon, if they could see you, Kinsley. Just imagining it…" She shook her head. "I knew I'd get watery, but don't you dare tell anyone it happened."

Doris pushed open the door.

The sun was setting. The stained-glass window behind the altar and pulpit glowing with subtle color and radiant light.

Kinsley noticed it, but her eyes were on Marcus, dressed in his tux, watching her as she stepped into the church.

His hazel eyes crinkled at the corners as he smiled, stepped forward to meet them, and held out his hand to take hers. She moved toward him, her heart thundering with joy.

Jay gave her a hug and a kiss on the cheek.

"I love you. Your dad loved you. Be happy, Kinsley. That is the best revenge." He stepped away, took a seat next to his wife and children.

Someone was sniffling.

Doris?

Kinsley didn't look. She was caught in Marcus's gaze, held captive as the pastor began to talk about marriage, about love, about the sacred covenant of those things.

God's design.

His way.

And He would be in this. Just as He had been in every part of Kinsley's life.

When it was time, she said, *I do*, her voice trembling, her heart soaring.

She *did*.

She *would*.

Every day. For always.

And then it was over and they were in each other's arms, sealing their vows with a kiss that made Rosie groan.

"No one told me there'd be kissing," she said.

The guests laughed.

Kinsley laughed, too, still looking into Marcus's eyes, and seeing everything she'd ever longed for there.

"I love you, Kinsley," he said, leaning down

to kiss the laughter from her lips. "Ready to start our lives together?"

"I thought you'd never ask," she said, taking his hand, lifting the hem of her skirts and walking back down the aisle.

Rosie pranced in front of them, Fitz walking beside her—all of it as precious and beautiful as the first ray of sunshine after a violent storm.

She had made it through.

They had made it through.

Together.

For always.

Kinsley would never stop being grateful for Marcus, for the family she finally had, the love she finally felt, the community she had become part of.

This was living.

This was thriving.

This was her life, and she would make every day a beautiful testimony to that.

For now and forever.

With Marcus by her side.

* * * * *

*If you enjoyed this story,
be sure to pick up these other exciting books
by Shirlee McCoy:*

Night Stalker
Gone
Dangerous Sanctuary
Lone Witness
Falsely Accused
Hidden Witness

*Available now from Love Inspired Suspense!
Find more great reads at
www.LoveInspired.com.*

Dear Reader,

During the winter, we long for the robin's cheerful bounce as it dances across the still-frozen ground. We search the landscape for daffodils bursting from the earth, and we wonder aloud if spring will ever come. When it does, we may forget how cold the days once were, how short the hours of sunshine and how desperate we were for warmth. I have purposed, these last few years, to not forget the hard, lean times of my life. When I have felt alone and undone, God was there. Showing His grace and power in the face of my seemingly insurmountable circumstances. May we praise Him as loudly in our winter hours as we do during the abundance of our spring's. He is always, always good.

I love hearing from readers. You can reach me at shirleermccoy@hotmail.com or connect with me on Facebook.

Blessings,

Shirlee McCoy

Get 4 FREE REWARDS!

We'll send you 2 FREE Books plus 2 FREE Mystery Gifts.

Love Inspired books feature uplifting stories where faith helps guide you through life's challenges and discover the promise of a new beginning

FREE Value Over **$20**

YES! Please send me 2 FREE Love Inspired Romance novels and my 2 FREE mystery gifts (gifts are worth about $10 retail). After receiving them, if I don't wish to receive any more books, I can return the shipping statement marked "cancel." If I don't cancel, I will receive 6 brand-new novels every month and be billed just $5.24 each for the regular-print edition or $5.99 each for the larger-print edition in the U.S., or $5.74 each for the regular-print edition or $6.24 each for the larger-print edition in Canada. That's a savings of at least 13% off the cover price. It's quite a bargain! Shipping and handling is just 50¢ per book in the U.S. and $1.25 per book in Canada.* I understand that accepting the 2 free books and gifts places me under no obligation to buy anything. I can always return a shipment and cancel at any time. The free books and gifts are mine to keep no matter what I decide.

Choose one: ☐ **Love Inspired Romance**
Regular-Print
(105/305 IDN GNWC)

☐ **Love Inspired Romance**
Larger-Print
(122/322 IDN GNWC)

Name (please print)

Address _____ Apt. #

City _____ State/Province _____ Zip/Postal Code

Email: Please check this box ☐ if you would like to receive newsletters and promotional emails from Harlequin Enterprises ULC and its affiliates. You can unsubscribe anytime.

Mail to the Harlequin Reader Service:
IN U.S.A.: P.O. Box 1341, Buffalo, NY 14240-8531
IN CANADA: P.O. Box 603, Fort Erie, Ontario L2A 5X3

Want to try 2 free books from another series! Call 1-800-873-8635 or visit www.ReaderService.com.

Get 4 FREE REWARDS!

We'll send you 2 FREE Books plus 2 FREE Mystery Gifts.

Harlequin Heartwarming Larger-Print books will connect you to uplifting stories where the bonds of friendship, family and community unite.

FREE Value Over **$20**